"Darrell and Mordisford," there was harsh mockery in Jonas's voice. "Malignants both. When such as they consort together, honest men had best beware."

"Then you may rest easily, Jonas," Charity said distinctly, "for what do you know of the ways of honest men?"

"You grow reckless, cousin," he said with a sneer, "and show us a glimpse of that intransigent temper and undutiful spirit which of late you have been learning to hide. Have you so soon forgotten what punishment I promised you if you defied me again?"

"Dear coz," she replied with dulcet mockery, "how could I ever forget anything you say to me?"

"This time, mistress, you have overreached yourself! Darrell Conyngton is not at hand to come to your aid."

"No, he is not!" She seized swiftly upon the only thing which might thwart his anger before it became ungovernable. "But remember, Jonas, that when he returns, there will be a reckoning to pay."

# Spring Will Come Again

## Sylvia Thorpe

A FAWCETT CREST BOOK

Fawcett Books, Greenwich, Connecticut

*SPRING WILL COME AGAIN*

THIS BOOK CONTAINS THE COMPLETE TEXT OF
THE ORIGINAL HARDCOVER EDITION.

A Fawcett Crest Book reprinted by arrangement with
Hutchinson Publishing Group.

ISBN: 0-449-23346-4

Printed in the United States of America

10  9  8  7  6  5  4  3  2  1

# 1

"BY GOD's grace, and by the will of the people of England, we are rid at last of the tyrant, the traitor, the Man of Blood, Charles Stuart has been tried, condemned and executed!"

As Charity Shenfield hurried across the moonlit, frost-whitened meadow, the terrible words repeated themselves endlessly in her mind. The cruel wars which had set friends and kindred one against the other were over, the Ironside army under Cromwell was the master of England, but old enmities burned still with undiminished fire, and nowhere more fiercely than in this Devonshire parish of Conyngton St John, in that rich countryside between Dartmoor and the sea.

The hatred which endured there was not altogether political, for with one exception the people were staunch for the King, but the exception was Jonas Shenfield of the Moat House, who was Charity's cousin and the richest man in the whole parish. He had not always been so. Before the Civil War the squire, Sir Darrell Conyngton, had been the most wealthy, as he was still the most respected, and the hatred which Shenfield bore him was rooted in their boyhood, when young Darrell had been so richly endowed with all those things Jonas himself most coveted—great wealth, rank, and personal popularity.

Youthful jealousy, aggravated by the troubles of the times, had since grown into something far more bitter and dangerous, and now, in spite of Jonas's zeal as a Puritan and an adherent of the victorious Parliament, his life was ruled by two passions only; hatred of Darrell Conyngton, and greed for even greater wealth and broader lands, that he might wield power where he could never hope to win liking.

Charity herself, penniless, half-French and orphaned at birth, had been brought up, with his own children, by her father's elder brother, Jonathan Shenfield, but since his death Jonas, as head of the family, had held over her a guardian's absolute authority. He had always disliked her, and her presence in his house was a constant irritation, but he suffered it gladly because in her he possessed a potent weapon with which to wound the man he hated above all others. That he wounded her also was an added satisfaction to him, just as it had given him pleasure that evening brutally to tell her of the killing of the captive King, for Charity clung fast to Royalist sympathies even in her kinsman's Puritan household. Now, on this bitter February night in 1649, numb and dazed with horror, she had slipped away from the Moat House and was hastening to the one person with whom she could share her desolation and despair, and in sharing it perhaps find for both of them some small measure of comfort.

She came at last to a fair-sized, timbered house set within the shelter of an encircling belt of trees. A startled man-servant answered her urgent knocking, but she brushed past him into the house without a word, and ran across the hall to enter a lighted room in its far side. She closed the door and stood for a moment leaning breathlessly against it, looking at the tall young man who had risen in astonishment from a chair before the fire. Then, as he came towards her, she, too, moved, and went unhesitatingly into his arms. They kissed with a kind of desperate hunger, for their meetings were few and perilous and brought as much pain as gladness, but after a few moments he put her away from him and looked searchingly into her face.

"What is it?' he said in a low anxious voice. "What has happened? No need to tell me it is some grievous thing."

Charity did not immediately reply, for suddenly the thing she had come to tell him seemed too appalling, too monstrous, to put into words. Darrell Conyngton had known the gay Court at Whitehall in the days before the war, and had marched and fought with Charles I through all his campaigns from Edgehill to the final defeat at Naseby, so that the news of the King's death must inevitably deal an even sharper, more personal blow to him than to her. She freed herself from his hold and moved to the fire, letting her cloak fall to the floor as she held out her hands to the blaze.

"What is it?" His voice was urgent now with misgiving. "No small matter could have prompted you to risk coming here. In God's name, Charity, tell me!"

She turned to face him, moving her hands in a little, helpless gesture. "I can find no words to soften the telling of it," she said wretchedly. "Darrell, they have killed the King!"

She saw his face whiten, and in his eyes the same stunned horror she herself felt. After a moment he said, his voice stricken and incredulous:

"They have murdered him?"

She shivered, and in a voice scarcely louder than a whisper, repeated the callous words with which her cousin had announced to his household the news of King Charles's death, words which now seemed to be branded indelibly upon her memory. Darrell listened with bitter contempt.

" 'By the will of the people of England,' " he repeated savagely. "Jonas should have said 'by the will of Oliver Cromwell and his army of fanatics'. Had the will of the people prevailed, His Majesty would be secure upon the throne again, his power curtailed, mayhap, but still King. No, whatever mummery of a trial they contrived to cloak their deed, every man who had a hand in this infamy is guilty of regicide, for there is no tribunal in the land with the powers to try the King. He and the realm are one."

They were silent for a while. Charity dropped to her knees beside the fire and leaned towards it, trying to dispel the deadly cold, like the chill of death itself, which still seemed to enfold her. The light from the leaping flames flickered across her face, a face of fine, bold outlines, black-browed and olive-skinned, framed by a close-fitting white cap which almost concealed her smooth black hair. She was dressed with Puritan severity, and her gown of dark grey homespun, with its apron and broad linen collar, might have been that of a servant. She was, in fact, treated like a servant in her kinsman's house, and her apparent indifference to the slights heaped upon her infuriated Jonas almost beyond endurance.

At last she said in a low voice, "Darrell, what will happen now?"

He came back to his chair and dropped dejectedly into it. "I believe that only one man alive could tell you that, for the Army rules England, and Cromwell rules the Army. This kingdom lies helpless, a drawn sword at its throat, and God alone knows how long it will be before that sword can be sheathed, or broken."

"What of the new young King?"

He sighed. "A lad not yet nineteen, in exile and all but penniless! Where is he to find resources great enough to defeat the Ironside army? Of a certainty, the Royalists here in England can do little."

She fell silent, recognising the truth of his words. The hopes of Royalist England had been centred upon the person of the King, who, defeated, imprisoned, stripped of the last vestige of temporal power, had yet during the past year come to represent to the mass of the people their only champion against the increasing power of the fanatical Army. Those hopes had even survived the cruel defeats of the Second Civil War, but now, with the death of the King, were finally extinguished. The Royalists, broken in arms, bled white by crippling fines and taxes, had been dealt the ultimate blow.

"I shall ride to Plymouth tomorrow," Darrell said suddenly. "There will be more to learn of the manner of His Majesty's death, and of what is now passing in London. I cannot rest until I know all that has befallen."

"Ah, Darrell, take care!" With a swift movement

Charity knelt upright to face him, and caught his hand in hers. "Is it prudent to go at such a time?"

"Why, love, what harm can come of it? I go but to discover such news as may be commonly learned, and I will bear myself circumspectly, I promise you."

"So say you now," she retorted, "but should some Roundhead chance to bait you, you are like to forget that firm resolve and take a high tone with him. I wish you would not go, for feeling is bound to run high in Plymouth at present." She paused, her loving, anxious gaze searching his face. "There are so many here, Darrell, who need you and depend upon you—I most of all!"

He looked at her, and a tenderness came into his face to banish the sternness which habitually dwelt there. It was a proud face, strong rather than handsome, the lean features framed by long hair of reddish-gold, the hazel eyes regarding the world with an expression of faint and bitter hauteur. Darrel was barely twenty-six, but the harshness of war and its aftermath, and of searing personal tragedy, had left him little of the lightheartedness of youth.

He came of a proud line, a family which had long been supreme in that particular corner of Devonshire, and it was not easy for him to see his wealth and lands diminished, his authority swept away into the hands of men violently opposed to everything he had been taught to revere, but the wars had robbed him of far more than influence and torture. He had seen his father die in battle, and by the time duty permitted him to return home, both his mother and the young wife to whom he was sincerely attached, even though the marriage had been arranged for him according to custom, were dead also. Even his little son had not survived infancy.[1]

Charity, who had known him nearly all her life, and loved him for as long as she had known him, understood better than anyone his bitterness and frustration, and how easily those feelings could be stirred to dangerous life. On the rare occasions when he visited Plymouth she lived in constant dread that he would be provoked into reckless action.

"I *must* go, Charity!" he said gently. "I must learn how this monstrous thing was accomplished and how the news has been received, and it will be long before such tidings reach us here. I will be discreet, I swear it!" He smiled a little, and with his free hand smoothed the furrow between her brows. "No need for these anxious looks, little one! I have lost too much not to hold doubly dear that which yet remains, and is the most precious thing of all. Did it not dissuade me last year from again taking up arms in the name of the King? Be sure then that it will keep me discreet in word and deed when I come to Plymouth, no matter how great the provocation. I know only too well that Jonas waits and watches for some opportunity to destroy me."

"If only we could see an end to it!" Charity rose abruptly to her feet and turned away, pressing her hands to her cheeks. "The days go by, and our hopes rise only to be dashed again, and now it seems that even hope is dead."

Darrell went quickly to take her in his arms, and she clung to him, hiding her face against his shoulder. She did not weep, for tears had never come easily to Charity Shenfield, but in her very silence there was a

1. Fair Shine the Day

longing and a despair he could not comfort because it was a reflection of his own. The barrier which Jonas's hatred had raised between them could be neither surmounted nor thrown down, and his own helplessness to overcome it was the cruellest defeat of all.

"There *is* a way," he said quietly. "A way we have spoken of before now. Many Royalists who found life here intolerable have sought refuge in exile. It would not be difficult to find some loyal fellow among the fisher-folk to put us across to France, and if the thing were well planned we could be away before Jonas suspected what was afoot."

"No!" She lifted her head sharply to look at him. "We agreed, did we not, that such flight was something we must never consider? You would scarcely be at sea before Jonas found some way of seizing the estate of Conyngton for himself, and you know how it would fare then with those who dwell here. You are their only defence against his malice and his greed, and we could find no happiness in each other if we deserted those who trust us."

"We may have no choice," he said somberly, "for while Jonas lives you might be under his authority and our marriage will never be permitted. It tears my heart to think of you in his house, slighted and misused while I am powerless to protect you. In flight lies our only sure hope."

"To leave England is to deliver Conyngton into his hands," she replied in a low voice. "I am not worthy of such sacrifice."

"Do you think there is anything in this world I would not relinquish for your sake?" he said huskily, and bent his head to kiss her. "Ah, Charity, my love!"

Her lips responded passionately to his, but after a moment she pulled herself from his arms and turned away, saying in a shaken voice: "It would not serve! We do but torture ourselves with temptation, for we both know in our hearts that we cannot so break faith and turn our backs upon duty and upon honour."

She stooped to pick up her cloak and wrapped it about her with trembling hands. Darrell said protestingly, "Must you go so soon?"

She sighed. "Is it not better so, for both our sakes?"

They looked wretchedly at each other, for of late it had been ever thus. Their meetings, schemed for and yearned for, came all too rarely, yet after the first rapturous moments they found themselves returning to the old arguments, the old, vain, desperate search for some way of escape from the hopeless situation in which they were trapped. At last Darrell said resignedly:

"I will walk back with you. Thus we may have at least a few minutes more together."

## II

A mile and a half away, on the other side of the hill, Jonas Shenfield sat with his mother before a roaring fire in the parlour of the Moat House. The old house, home of the Shenfield family for generations, stood alone in a hollow between two wooded hills, but of late it had been isolated from its neighbours by more than mere location, for in that staunchly Royalist community Jonas Shenfield's austerely Puritan household was looked upon with loathing.

Jonas, having announced the news of King Charles's

execution to his household when it assembled for evening prayers, had since been holding forth at length to his mother upon the boundless advantages to England in having finally rid itself of Kings. Elizabeth Shenfield listened in doting silence, her gaze dwelling upon him with fond, maternal pride. He was a stocky, powerfully-built young man in his middle twenties, with the fair-haired, blue-eyed good looks common to all the Shenfields except Charity, though anyone less besotted than his mother would have perceived that it was a harsh, humourless face where pride and intolerance were plainly written.

His dress was dark-coloured and of the utmost plainness, as became a devout Puritan, but fashioned as always of the finest materials. Jonas's comfortable patrimony had been augmented by the fortune left to him by his mother's two brothers, wealthy merchants of Plymouth, and by his own inherent shrewdness. Nor had his marriage a year before failed to increase his resources, for his bride, the youngest daughter of a prosperous alderman, had brought him a handsome dowry.

"Did you mark, my son," Elizabeth asked with relish when at length he fell silent, "how Charity blenched and faltered when you told how justice had been done, and the tyrant executed? For a moment it seemed that she was like to swoon."

"Yes, I marked it!" There was a grim satisfaction in Jonas's voice. "For the most part she has learned to remain impassive under any provocation, so it was all the more gratifying to witness her dismay tonight."

"She was ever a sly, deceitful creature," Mrs Shenfield said vindictively. "A wayward, defiant brat from the day she was born, and no attempts of mine to school her ever brought her to a proper sense of gratitude to us for giving her a home. But there, bad blood will out, depend upon it! Her father was a dissolute, roistering rogue, fit husband for the black-eyed French wanton he married. The girl has inherited his wildness and her mother's loose, foreign ways, and it would be a glad day if we could rid ourselves of her for good."

"Why, madam, so we could, by permitting her to marry Darrell Conyngton, but that is the very course to which she would like to provoke me, and I would rather be burdened with her for the rest of her days. It pleases me to deny him that which he most desires, and besides, I have no wish to see an heir to Conyngton."

"Then find a husband for her elsewhere! It would be worth the cost of a small dowry to be rid of her at last, and if you moved your household to Plymouth for a space, the marriage could take place before Conyngton discovered what you intended. You are her guardian! No one could question your right to bestow her hand as you see fit."

"Do you suppose I have not thought of it?" Jonas stared moodily into the fire. "But the disadvantages might well outweigh the gain. Conyngton is so besotted with her that he will never marry another woman while she is free, but if I so placed her beyond his reach, it might be a different matter." He broke off, slewing himself round in his chair as a servant came softly into the room. "Well, Stotewood, what now?"

Daniel Stotewood advanced and bowed. He was a gaunt, sallow-faced young man with the gleam of fanaticism in his pale eyes, and a manner servile to those above him but insolent and overbearing to his inferiors. Like all the indoor servants, he was a native of Plymouth, and though ostensibly Jonas's body-servant, he had in the course of time become also his henchman, spy and confidant. No man stood closer in Jonas Shenfield's counsels, and none understood better how to curry favour with him.

"May it please you, sir," he announced with unconcealed satisfaction, "Miss Charity left the house with some stealth as soon as prayers were over."

Jonas was silent for a moment, looking at him beneath frowning brows, and then said shortly, "Whither went she?"

"Through the stableyard, sir, and across the meadow towards the brook. That was not long since. If you wish, I can follow and fetch her back."

Jonas shook his head. "No, let her go!" He saw that his mother was about to protest, and added quickly to forestall her: "Keep watch for my cousin, and when she returns, come to me again."

He waved the man away, and as soon as they were alone again Mrs Shenfield said irritably: "What ails you, Jonas? You know, do you not, whither the sly wench has gone?"

"Aye, to the Dower House!" Jonas leaned back in his chair, complacently smoothing the rich cloth of his doublet. "I knew that she would waste no time in hurrying to tell Darrell Conyngton of Charles Stuart's execution, and my one regret is that I cannot be by to see him receive the news."

His mother looked unconvinced. "It is not just tonight, Jonas, that she flouts your authority and disobeys your express commands. She meets Conyngton at other times also, and the whole parish knows it."

He shrugged. "What matter? I knew when I gave that command that it would be impossible to enforce unless I kept her a close prisoner here. Let these rustic fools believe, if they choose, that I am duped by the supposed secrecy of such meetings. Only you and I, and Daniel Stotewood, know differently."

"Did you know that when Charity walks through the village, men doff their hats and women curtsy as though she were in fact the squire's lady?"

"I know it, and I shall not forget. The time will come when they regret that insolence."

Mrs Shenfield sighed. "So said you nearly two years since, when Darrell Conyngton first came home after the wars. We looked then to see you become the squire within a twelvemonth."

"I shall become so yet, madam, make no doubt of that!" he replied grimly. "Yet it is true I thought to have achieved my purpose by now. The estate had so fallen into decay it seemed certain he would be obliged to sell more and more of it in order to maintain the shrinking fragment that remained to him, but save for those lands which came into my possession at the time he compounded, he has parted with not a single acre. Nay, more! That which he still possesses has even recovered some part of its former prosperity."

"He must have resources, my son, of which you know nothing."

"Aye, so he must, but whence come they? How can an accursed malignant like Conyngton find the means to set his affairs in order?"

"If you could learn that," his mother remarked

shrewdly, "you might find in the knowledge the weapon you seek to destroy him."

"Mayhap!" Jonas stretched out a booted foot to thrust back a toppling log. "Find such a weapon I will, thus, or through Charity, or by some other means, but if I am to prevail I must be content to bide my time. Patience, Mother! Patience is all!"

III

Darell and Charity walked together across the moon-silvered park. Behind them the Dower House lay hidden among the trees, but away to their left, on the very crest of the hill, the burned-out skeleton of a great mansion loomed starkly against the sky from a dark wilderness of garden. This was Coyngton, which had been the home of the family of that name until plundered and burned by Roundhead soldiers. Now the ruins brooded, silent and forsaken, like a wordless comment upon all the sorrow and destruction of the past seven years.

Charity saw Darrell glance involuntarily towards them, and slipped her hand into his, stabbed anew by sadness, and by hopeless longing for all that was lost. The Conyngton of her childhood had been a happy place, rich in love and laughter, the warm heart of her world. Now only a memory remained.

"Six years ago, when that vile deed was done," Darrell said bitterly, "it seemed that nothing worse could befall. Well for us then that we could not foresee this day!"

The low-spoken words were charged with pain and anger, for he had been passionately devoted to his beautiful home. To him it had been "the fairest place on earth," and when in the summer of 1642 he and his father led their men to fight for Church and King, it was Conyngton also that the young Darrell had ridden forth to defend; Conyngton, his heritage and his pride. He had returned to find the beloved place a crumbling, blackened ruin, and only the Dower House left to give him shelter. Charity knew what distress every sight of the ruins caused him, for she, too, had loved Conyngton, and felt it to be more truly her home than the Moat House could ever be. Her happiest hours had been spent there, and Darrell and his parents given her the only real affection her bleak childhood had known.

"The land remains, Darrell," she said gently at length, "and one day Conyngton will rise again. We must never cease to believe that."

"If Jonas has his way, even my remaining lands will be taken from me," Darrell replied grimly. "His wealth and influence grow as mine diminish, and it would not be difficult for a man in his position to twist the law to his own advantage against a defeated enemy. It needs but one false step upon my part."

"Then you must be ever on your guard, my dear, against taking such a step. Already he is suspicious, and marvels that you have not found it necessary to sell even more of the estate."

"Yet the day is bound to come when I am obligated to do so!" Darrell's tone was bitter. "Even the jewels will not last for ever, and when the last of them has gone, I shall have no choice."

She did not reply, for the truth he had just uttered was too well known to them to warrant further comment. The Conyngton jewels, saved by an ingenious trick from the destruction which had engulfed the house, hoarded secretly through years of war, had proved to be the salvation of the estate. Unobtrusively disposed of from time to time, they had provided the money so sorely needed to repair the ravages of neglect and decay, and it was solely due to them that no more of the Conyngton lands had fallen into Jonas Shenfield's greedy grasp. What would happen when that source of gold was finally drained dry, Charity did not care to contemplate.

"We must have faith," she said resolutely. "To lose that is to lose all else besides."

"Still so valiant, little one?" he said gently. "Upon my life, I think yours is the bravest spirit I have ever known!"

She shook her head, determined to conceal from him how much it cost her to speak with such firmness. She had no patience with women who wept and clung, and she was already ashamed of her recent surrender to despair. So she smiled and pressed his hand, and with head held high walked on beside him.

The parkland ended at a thick belt of woodland clothing the steep hillside, but a narrow path wound downwards between the trees. At the foot of the hill, a brawling brook marked the boundary between Conyngton and Shenfield land, and in the distance could be glimpsed the roof and chimneys of the Moat House. On the bank of the stream Charity halted.

"We had best part here," she said. "I believe I was seen as I left the house, and Jonas or his minion may be on the watch for me."

He frowned. "Better then that I come with you. If Jonas knows that you have been with me, I will not leave you to face his anger alone."

Charity shook her head, smiling wryly in the darkness. "Dear heart, do you not yet know the tortuous paths his mind follows? He knows we meet, but seeks by pretending ignorance to preserve his dignity in the eyes of others."

"Jonas does not change!" There was anger and contempt in Darrell's voice. "Braggart, coward and bully he ever was and ever will be! I cannot be easy, knowing the authority he holds over you."

"He will not harm me, Darrell, for in spite of everything he fears you still."

"As well he may!" Darrell said grimly. "Should he harm you, my little one, I would kill him for it, no matter what the cost."

"Hush, my dear!" She laid her finger lightly across his lips. "He will move against me only in the small, malicious ways I have learned to bear with. Now kiss me farewell and let me go, for already I have been absent too long."

Reluctantly he did so, and stood watching her go from him across the frost-whitened meadow. For all her brave words, he knew how she suffered beneath her kinsman's malice, and because she was more dear to him than anything in the world, bitter anger at his own inability to shield her from it rose again within him. In that dark hour his own sorrows and frustrations seemed inextricably confused with the greater tragedy which had engulfed their lives, and, leaning against the tree beneath which he stood, he buried his face in the crook of his arm, shaken by a passion of fury and despair.

## IV

Reaching the Moat House, Charity slipped quietly through the gate to the stableyard and barred it behind her. As she crossed the yard towards the door which gave access to the kitchen quarters a dig stirred and growled somewhere in the darkness, but when she whispered its name, quietened down again at the sound of a familiar voice. The door, which she had also left unlocked, swung open at her touch, and she recoiled with a stifled, involuntary cry, for just within, where the light of a single tallow candle cast its feeble light, Daniel Stotewood was standing. He grinned at her obvious discomfiture, and Charity, stepping in and closing the door, said angrily:

"Why lurk you here? Have you not duties to occupy you?"

"My present duty, mistress, is to keep watch for you, but my master is ill pleased that you so neglect yours."

"Then let him tell me so himself," she retorted, and made as though to pass by, only to find her way barred by an outstretched arm.

"His lady had need of you while you were abroad."

Her brows lifted. "With the house full of idle servants, Mrs Jonas is not likely to have suffered by my absence. Now let me pass! It is not for you to censure me."

"Is it not?" Stotewood's voice was suddenly harsh, and he leaned towards her, the light from the candle casting sinister shadows across his gaunt, fanatical face. "My master cannot or will not see the evil which festers in his house! He turns aside from knowledge of it and lets you go your wanton way, but the reckoning will come, make no mistake of that. Damnation and hell-fire await those who yield themselves to the lusts of the flesh!"

Charity drew back, looking at him with the utmost contempt. "If there is evil in this house, Stotewood, it is not I who bring it. 'Tis you and your master, with your professions of godliness and your unclean minds which see sin in all things; who deny the mercy of God and think only of His vengeance, yet give your loyalty to those who have wantonly shed the blood of God's anointed."

"Be silent, woman! Have you no shame, that you dare to speak the name of the Lord thus when you have come straight from the arms of your lover? Do not think that your wickedness is known only to you and to him! Such evil-doing is an abomination in the eyes of the Lord, and sets the imprint of Satan upon this godly household."

Quite suddenly Charity's patience deserted her. She was still sick with shock at the news of the King's death, her feelings further lacerated by the brief, tormented time she had spent with Darrell, and to stand here in this cold, shadowy passage while Daniel Stotewood spat out his venom was more than she could endure. Making no attempt to disguise her disgust and detestation, she said coldly:

"If you have a message from your master, deliver it, and if not, stand aside and preach to me no more. You are not chaplain of my kinsman's household yet."

"Aye, mock me, you Jezebel!" The man's harsh voice was shaking with rage. "Stand there in your sinful pride and mock at the Lord's elect! The day is not far distant when that pride shall be cast down, and you and the malignant Conyngton be destroyed, as the Man of Blood has been destroyed in blood!"

He gripped her arm as he spoke, thrusting his pallid, distorted countenance to within a few inches of her own, and like a fury she turned upon him, striking aside the importunate hand with all the force at her command. Her eyes were blazing with anger, but in strange contrast to them her voice was low and controlled.

"Dare to lay a hand on me again, sirrah, and as God is my witness, you will be sorry for it! I am not answerable for my conduct to any prying lackey who skulks in the shadows to learn what is no concern of his, and if you think your master at fault in his bearing towards me, go prate of it to him and see what answer it earns you."

She thrust him aside and walked quickly away from him along the passage. Daniel Stotewood stood staring after her, his pale eyes narrowed and his lips thin and ugly with rage, until she had passed from sight, and then with a gesture of uncontrollable fury he struck the guttering candle from its shelf to the stone floor, and ground its feeble glimmer to extinction beneath his heel.

# 2

NEXT afternoon, when it was beginning to grow dark, Charity sat in a great bedchamber at the Moat House, where Ellen, Jonas's wife, lay propped against pillows in the big four-poster which, like the rest of the room, had been furnished with new and splendid hangings for her lying-in. She was just seventeen, a small, gentle girl who looked lost and child-like in the shadows of the vast bed. Now and then she glanced wistfully at her companion, as though she would have liked to talk, but although Charity was a mere dependant ranking not far above the upper servants, Ellen was still a little in awe of this seemingly aloof young woman with her air of calm self-possession.

Charity herself was completely unaware of Ellen's regard, even of her presence in the room. Her busy needle flashed with swift, unthinking skill, just as her foot expertly maintained the rhythmic rocking of the wooden cradle at her side, for though her body sat dutifully in her kinsman's house, in thought and spirit she was away across the twilight fields.

The week-old infant in the cradle stirred and whimpered and then, despite the rocking, broke into a full-throated wail. Charity laid aside her sewing and got up, but as she lifted the child, Ellen said fretfully:

"Give him to me, if you please."

Just for an instant Charity hesitated, and then with the faintest lifting of her brows, an almost imperceptible shrug, laid the baby in his mother's arms and moved away to the window, where the cold, blue dusk seemed to press against the panes. She stood staring out, while the baby continued to wail, his cries becoming louder and more insistent.

At last, with a sharp, exasperated movement, she drew the curtains together and returned to the bed. Without speaking, she took the child again and began to walk to and fro, rocking him gently until his screams subsided. Ellen watched resentfully, tears of vexation rising to her eyes.

"It is passing strange," she said querulously at length, "that you should always succeed in quieting him when I cannot. I vow he seems more content in your arms than in mine!"

"And you bear me a grudge therefore!" A note of amusement sounded in Charity's calm voice. "There is no need! Jonathan is your first-born, and you are timid and over-anxious. That will pass, believe me!"

Ellen shifted irritably against her pillows. "You are full of wise counsel, cousin, which I could more readily accept if it came from one who was herself a wife and mother. In truth, I know not why my husband should have chosen *you* to be nurse to our son."

"Because of all his household, I am the one most fitted for the task," Charity replied crisply. "I marvel that no one here has yet informed you that this is not the first time I have found myself with a babe to rear."

Ellen's blue eyes widened with astonishment. She had spent the first months of her married life at Jonas's house in Plymouth, her own native town, and had only been brought to his country home as the time of her confinement approached. There was still a good deal she did not know about his family, but she found it hard to credit a revelation such as this. She said incredulously:

"You have a child?"

For the first time Charity's eyes were raised from contemplation of the infant in her arms. They were dark eyes, deeply set, which could at times flash with a spirit oddly at variance with her usual discreet bearing, but just now they were full of mockery.

"I *had* a child," she corrected calmly. "Oh, I did not bear him, but he was mine from the hour he first drew breath. His mother died giving birth to him in this house six years ago." She looked down at the baby, now sleeping peacefully once more, and when she spoke again there was a deep wistfulness in her voice. "He was a frail mite, though, carried in sorrow and borne in loneliness and terror. You are fortunate, cousin, in this sturdy lad of yours."

Ellen stared at her, remembering the time when England had been in the early months of the bitter conflict between King and Parliament. She had been a child then in Plymouth, the town itself a Roundhead stronghold in a countryside which was for the most part fiercely Royalist, and she wondered what tragedy of those days lay behind Charity's disclosure. She could not find the courage to ask, but instead said with diffident sympathy:

"Did the child not live, Cousin Charity?"

27

She saw a curious change come over the other woman's face, as though she had once more withdrawn into herself and was already regretting that she had revealed so much. Charity said curtly:

"His span was little more than four brief years. He drowned in the moat yonder." She laid the baby in Ellen's arms again and turned away. "It is time for your cordial. I will fetch it from the still-room."

The door closed behind her and Ellen shivered, seeing in her mind's eye the moat from which the house took its name. This was now no more than a broad, deep pool, separated from the gardens by an ancient, crumbling wall and a ruined tower, but it was easy to picture a small child being swallowed by its dark and silent depths.

As she cuddled her baby closer, loneliness and depression swept over her in a chilling flood. She thought of her parents in Plymouth, of the married brothers and sisters there, and, most wistfully of all, of her eldest and best-loved brother, Tom. A seafarer who had been away from England for more than a year, Captain Pennan was not even aware of her marriage, and Ellen longed desperately for him to come home. She had lived all her life in the busy seaport town, and to her the Moat House seemed a grim and solitary place. Even now, in her warm, candlelit room with the curtains drawn against the winter nightfall, she was depressingly aware of the silent countryside stretching all around, alien and faintly menacing under the darkening sky.

Charity, meanwhile, measuring out cordial in the stillroom, did so absently, a frown between her black brows. The painful memories which had been stirred to life the first time Ellen's new-born son was laid in her arms grew sharper with each passing day, and she knew that this was what Jonas had intended. He was a master of the small cruelty, the sly, malicious wounding against which she had no defence save the veneer of calm indifference which, slowly and painfully over the years, she had learned to assume.

She replaced the flask of cordial in the cupboard, closed the door and rested her forehead against it, trying to shake off the depression that possessed her. Sometimes she felt that she could no longer endure Jonas's harsh scorn, his mother's constant, unjustified complaints, or the dreariness of life in this house which had become less a home than a prison. Yet endure them she must, for there was no escape.

A light footstep sounded, and Sarah, Jonas's pretty young sister, came into the room. Charity turned quickly, but Sarah had seen that brief surrender to despair, and because there was a strong bond of affection between them, her immediate desire was to offer comfort. She came quickly to her side.

"Dear coz," she said gently, "try not to grieve, hard though it is to bear. This is what my brother desires, to break your spirit with sorrow, and with cruel memories of what is past."

"Do I not know it?" Charity straightened her shoulders and tried to smile. "Be easy, Sarah! Though it rend my heart every time I take Ellen's baby in my arms, Jonas shall not know it, and if he hopes for some show of resentment at the task he has laid upon me, he will be disappointed. That satisfaction, at least, I can deny him."

"Then 'tis the only satisfaction which at present he

*is* denied," Sarah said gloomily. "All else goes in his favour. He is still giving thanks for the grievous news that reached us yesterday."

Charity sighed. "It is long indeed since any joyful tidings came to this house—joyful, that is, for any save rebels and traitors. Did not our hearts lift last summer when we heard that men had once more taken up arms in the name of the King, but what followed? Cromwell and his accursed Army crushed all our hopes in a matter of months."

Sarah looked alarmed. Charity's passionate devotion to the Royal cause was no secret, but it was a devotion which of late had seldom been expressed in words.

"Charity, have a care what you say! If one of the servants were to hear you and carry tales to my brother—"

"Jonas knows well enough where my loyalty lies, and has known these many years. Since before he turned Puritan to make certain of inheriting his uncles' fortune."

"Know it he may, but for his servants to hear such thoughts spoken aloud in this house is something he would not overlook. For them to hear it said that he turned Puritan for the sake of gain he would never forgive. What ails you, Charity? It is usually I who need to be warned against an indiscreet tongue."

"Yes, you are right," Charity said wearily. "Your brother's malice begins to do its work, and irks me into voicing thoughts better left unspoken. You do well to set me on my guard, for I dare not let Jonas provoke me into giving him an excuse for punishment. I have had to bear his spite all my life, and should have armoured myself against the pinpricks of it by now."

Early on a bleak and cheerless morning nearly a week later, Charity was hurrying across the park towards the ruined manor. Daylight had come tardily that day, and an icy north wind was roaring down from the Dartmoor to scourge the defenceless countryside, but Charity's heart was light because Darrell had come home unscathed from Plymouth. News of his return had been brought to her the previous night by Polly, the little maidservant who helped with the work in the nursery.

Polly had been at the Moat House only since the previous summer, but this was long enough for her to have found a sweetheart among the younger farm-labourers, and since this youth was a native of the parish, she had learned from him a good deal about local loyalties and rivalries. Charity always treated her kindly, and had even nursed her through a brief illness soon after her arrival from Plymouth, and as a result Polly was ranged firmly upon her side against the master of the house. It had afforded her vast satisfaction to join forces with her swain to establish a means of communication between Charity and Darrell.

This enabled them to meet occasionally, usually in the gatehouse or gardens at Conyngton. These lay nearer to the Moat House than Darrell's present home, though this was not Charity's only reason for fearing to visit the Dower House itself. The loyalty of the servants there, and of the village folk, was beyond question, but in so small and close-knit a community gossip was inevitable, and she knew that if ever Jonas were obliged to acknowledge her disobedience, even the bitter-sweet consolation of stolen meetings would be denied them.

The gatehouse, set in the high wall surrounding the gardens, had escaped the fire which destroyed the mansion and its outbuildings, though its tiny windows had been smashed and the great, iron-studded doors cast down from their hinges in the general fury of destruction. The little room where the gatekeeper had once dwelt, and to which Charity now came to meet Darrell, was bare of furniture and littered with dead leaves and broken twigs, but its stout walls provided a measure of shelter and a certain sense of privacy.

He was waiting there for her, and she clung to him as though until that moment the fears she had felt for him during his absence had not been wholly laid to rest. Anxiously studying his face, she read there a weariness of the spirit which smote her to the heart.

"Dear love," she said gently, "what news do you bring?"

"Little enough that we did not already know," he replied with a sigh. "The regicides did indeed subject His Majesty to some mockery of a trial, and though no precedent for such a thing could be found, Cromwell and the Army cared nothing for that. They had already determined upon the killing of the King."

"They have killed one King," Charity said slowly, "and yet by that very deed have made his son King in his stead. Thus, surely, they defeat their own evil purpose, since His Majesty is free and beyond their reach."

"For us, and thousands like us, that is a simple truth, though the young King will need more than silent loyalty and secret toasts to his health and prosperity to bring him back to the throne. The regicides deny that he has any rights in the kingdom. I heard it said, by one who was recently in London, that even a statue of our martyred sovereign has been cast down, and in its place inscribed the words "exit the tyrant, the last of the Kings." God send a day when that prediction be proven false."

Charity shivered, and drew her cloak more closely about her. "May that day come soon, though I fear a miracle will be needed to bring it about!"

"A miracle in truth!" Darrell turned sharply away from her and stood staring through the shattered window. There was harsh desperation in his voice. "And such evidence of Divine mercy has been withheld from us these many years. Meanwhile men strive to do what they can in the name of duty and of loyalty, yet what *can* we do now? In the straits to which we are reduced, even the consolation of action is denied us."

She watched with loving, troubled eyes, yearning to offer comfort and encouragement yet knowing there was none to give. A woman learned hard and bitter lessons in time of war. Her man might ride away to battle, but she must bide at home and continue the small, day-to-day tasks which must be performed no matter what cataclysm engulfed the land, what dread or sadness filled her own heart. From the cruel experiences of the past seven years Charity, and countless women like her, had learned perforce the patience to bear the burden of the endless, empty days. Men like Darrell, proud even in defeat, inured now to the dangers of war and ready to risk them again for the Cause, had that lesson yet to learn, and her heart ached for him now because she knew it would be the hardest lesson of all.

"We can do nothing," she said after a while, and in spite of all the loving compassion she felt, her voice was cool and level and faintly challenging. "Nothing save preserve what is left to us, husband it carefully against the day when action will again be possible, and meanwhile so bear ourselves that we provoke neither the anger nor the malice of those who are now ascendant over us."

Darrell swung round to face her again, a glint of anger in his eyes. "Do you presume, Charity, to teach me my duty?"

"No." she retorted quietly, "to teach you wisdom, and to point to you the path, the only path, which lies ahead. It may not be to your liking, but that is no fault of mine."

There was silence for a moment, silence which hovered perilously on the brink of a quarrel, for Darrell, his feelings taut and frayed by things he had heard in Plymouth, and by the general air of triumph in that predominantly Roundhead town, was ready to strike out even at Charity. She confronted him calmly, neither angry nor defiant, and after a few seconds his expression relaxed a little and he said ruefully:

"You are as forthright now, are you not, as when you were a wayward imp of a child—and as ready to set your will against mine?"

She nodded. "When it is needful, Darrell! It will be an ill day indeed when I fear to speak my mind frankly to you."

"Even if it moves me to anger?"

"Even so! What, would you have me afraid of you?"

34

"No!" He spoke quickly, putting out his hands to her, and she shook back her cloak to put her own into them. "Never that, little one! If ever I see fear of me in *your* eyes, I shall know that I am lost indeed."

"You may see fear *for* you reflected there," she replied gravely. "You will strive for patience, will you not, and do nothing to place yourself in danger? Believe, as I do, that when the time comes, God will show us the way."

"I will try," he said quietly. "It will not be easy, but—I will try. And when the time does come . . ." He paused, and she felt a swift stab of alarm as she read in his face the very impatience he was trying to deny.

"Darrell," she said urgently, "promise me one thing! Promise me that you will embark upon no course of action against our enemies without first telling me of it." He looked doubtful, and she added in a pleading voice: "Dear heart, our lives are bound together as one! I ask only that you do not risk that life without my knowledge."

For a moment or two he remained silent, looking down into the dark eyes raised so earnestly to his. Tall though he was, they were only an inch or two below the level of his own.

"I will make you that promise," he said at length, "though if such a course of action offers I cannot undertake to hold aloof from it at your behest. But I swear that I will tell you of it."

With that she had to be content, and draw what reassurance she could from the thought that there was at present little likelihood of putting the promise to the test. If a chance to serve the King in any way did offer itself, she knew that Darrell would take it without hesitation. The previous year, during the short, disastrous campaign of the Second Civil War, she had only with the utmost difficulty dissuaded him from once more taking up arms. Events had proved her instinct to be sound, but she knew that he had never quite forgiven himself for what he regarded as a failure to keep faith. She even wondered sometimes whether he had forgiven her.

### III

That meeting in the gatehouse was to be their last for several weeks, during which they saw each other only in church, when Charity was surrounded by her kinfolk. She and Darrell, like the rest of the village, went reluctantly to church now, for they disliked and distrusted Dr Malperne, the Puritan preacher who had been granted the living when the old parson, Dr Flagge, was deprived of it. Parson Flagge had been a friend to them all, but his successor owed his position to Jonas Shenfield's patronage, and this alone was sufficient to set every inhabitant of Conyngton St John against him.

On a mild, bright Sunday towards the middle of March when already a hint of spring was in the air, Ellen went with her husband and his family to church. This was her first visit to the village, for when Jonas brought her from Plymouth her pregnancy had been too far advanced, and the winter weather too severe for her to make the two-mile journey, and now the prospect of going at last beyond the immediate confines of the Moat House filled her with anticipation. There was colour in her cheeks and an excited sparkle in her eyes, and she looked eagerly about her as the great family coach lumbered precariously down the hill and along the gently curving village street.

Most of the thatched cottages were clustered about a triangular green, with the church facing them on the opposite side of the road. The churchyard was skirted by the small river, and beyond it could be glimpsed the great wheel of the water-mill, while at the far end of the village, in front of the Conyngton Arms, the road turned sharply to cross an old stone bridge before winding on its way to Plymouth.

"How pretty the village is!" Ellen exclaimed. "Yet I thought it a dismal place when I passed through it last autumn."

"The ugliness of sin lurks here as it lurks everywhere," Mrs Shenfield rebuked her sharply. "Turn your thoughts to less worldly matters, Ellen, as befits one about to enter the house of the Lord."

Ellen flushed scarlet, and Charity pressed her lips tightly together to keep back a barbed retort. Passionately responsive herself to beauty of any kind, she found the Puritan obsession for coupling it always with evil, and for turning ugliness into a virtue, an affront to her deepest beliefs, but she knew better than to show it. The fact that she was permitted to ride to church with the other ladies of the family was one of the few concessions granted to her on the grounds of kinship, and her aunt would seize gladly upon any excuse for banishing her to walk with the servants.

Groups of villagers were walking along the street and through the churchyard, but when the coach halted at the lych-gate and Jonas, who had been riding beside it, came to help the ladies to alight, the people drew back and waited in sullen silence for the Shenfields to go in. Only for Charity were there smiles and friendly glances.

The church was small and very old, its interior stripped bare of ornament and whitewashed after the Puritan fashion, the sunlight falling harshly through windows of plain glass. Jonas and his family had scarcely taken their places when the sound of spurred boots rang again on the stone floor, and Ellen, glancing cautiously sideways, saw a tall, russet-haired man in black velvet come into the church. From his dress and his assured bearing she guessed that this was the Cavalier squire of whom she had heard, and was surprised to see that he was young. For some reason she had pictured Sir Darrell Conyngton as a much older man.

She was a devout young woman and the sermon occupied her whole attention, but later, when the congregation filed out into the sunshine, she became aware again of an atmosphere of intense hostility. On every side she saw blank, unsmiling faces, and though women curtsied and men uncovered as Jonas and his family passed by, the courtesy was grudgingly paid. Shocked and disturbed, her earlier pleasure quite banished, she walked beside her husband along the path to the lych-gate, where Sir Darrell Conyngton stood talking to a stalwart young countryman. They stepped aside to let the Shenfields pass, and though the squire bowed to the ladies no word was spoken, and Ellen saw in his proud, stern face a bleak lack of expression even more disquieting than the antagonism of the villagers.

The memory of it weighed heavily upon her during the homeward journey, posing an uneasy, unanswerable question. By the time the Moat House was reached she had sunk to the very depths of despondency, and the big, gloomy hall, cold after the sunlight in spite of a blazing fire, seemed to close round her like a prison. She sank wearily on to a stool and covered her face with her hands, trying to hide the tears she could no longer hold back.

"What ails you, Ellen?" Mrs Shenfield's sharp voice held more impatience than concern. "Was the journey to the village too much for you?"

Ellen shook her head without looking up, and Elizabeth uttered an exasperated exclamation. Jonas, who had gone to stand with his back to the fire, regarded his wife with a frown, while Charity, already at the foot of the stairs on her way to the nursery, halted and looked round, and then came slowly back.

"Are you ill, madam?" Jonas demanded brusquely. Ellen shook her head again, murmuring something indistinguishable, and he added more sharply: "Then pray have the courtesy to look at me when I address you! If you are not ailing, what is the reason for this foolish conduct?"

This time Ellen did look up, her cheeks streaked with tears. The months of loneliness since coming to the Moat House, her bitter disappointment at the hostility she had sensed among their neighbours, had wrought her to such a pitch that at last she could find the courage to voice the plea she had never before dared to make. In a voice which broke piteously into a sob, she said desperately:

"I am so unhappy here! Now that the spring has come, please, please may we not go back to Plymouth?"

He did not reply at once, but considered her for a

few moments with a look of frowning displeasure before which she shrank in dismay. Then he said cruelly:

"No, madam, we may not! The house in Plymouth serves me very well while I conduct my business, but this is my family home and it is here that my children will be reared. Understand that, and let me hear no more complaints of this kind."

"Unseemly talk, indeed!" his mother added waspishly. "What fault, pray, have you to find with the Moat House?"

Ellen, already unnerved by Jonas's harsh rebuke, flinched at this attack from one whom she feared almost as much as she feared her husband. Already she was regretting the temerity to which dismay had prompted her.

"Why, none, madam, save that it is more lonely than I have been used to," she stammered, "but in the village there is hatred. I could feel it all around us as we came from church."

"What, do you pay heed to the black looks of a pack of rustics?" Mrs Shenfield retorted scornfully. "They are but ignorant fools, stirred to dislike of us by those who think to profit from it. Is it because of this that you would go scurrying back to Plymouth?"

Ellen swallowed nervously, wishing with all her heart that she had never provoked this scene, for since coming to the Moat House she had realized that she would never be mistress there while Elizabeth Shenfield lived, and that against her decrees, and Jonas's, there could be no defiance, no appeal. Afraid to persist, yet more afraid to surrender without attempting to justify herself, she said faintly:

"What of the squire, Sir Darrell Conyngton, who

looked on us this day with a face like stone? Is he, too, to be dismissed as an ignorant fool?"

"He is worse than that!" Jonas's voice throbbed with such savage vindictiveness that her glance returned to him in terror. "An accursed malignant who would ride roughshod over honest men, and taint the Church with the idolatorous practices of Rome!"

"That is a foul lie!" The intervention came, unexpectedly, from Charity, and Ellen, looking at her in astonishment, saw that her chin was up and her eyes blazing with anger. "The Conyngtons have ever been true to the Established Church, just as they have always been loyal to the King, yet for that you dare to name him a malignant. Do you not know that every man and woman in this parish looks upon *you* as a regicide?"

For a fraction of a second Jonas glared at her as though this open defiance was something he could scarcely credit, and then he strode forward and struck her open-handed across the face with such force that she staggered. His own face was pallid with fury.

"I am well aware of the rebellion which seethes in this benighted place," he said in a voice that shook with rage, "and in the fullness of time it shall be put down, but meanwhile I will have obedience and respect in this house at least. Defy me but once more in this fashion and you shall have a whip laid across your back. Now get to your work, and you, madam"—this to his wife—"go look to my son! I have had a surfeit of this folly!"

"It is not folly!" Sarah, who had rushed to Charity's side and flung her arms around her, now turned upon her brother as though she could no longer contain herself. "We *are* hated by all the good folk in the village, and 'tis you we have to thank for that. You provoked this hatred and now we must all suffer for it, as though it were some foul disease which infects every one of us."

"Sarah, be silent!" The menace in Jonas's voice brought home to the girl the enormity of her offence. "If aught infects this household it is the plague of disobedience and disrespect, and I know well enough whence that springs!" His baleful glance rested once more upon Charity as she stood leaning on Sarah's shoulder, a hand to her cheek, and then he looked again at his sister. "As for you, my girl, it is time you had a husband to check your waywardness. I must give thought to it! Now get out of my sight, all three of you, and see that you pray for humility, and a proper repentance for your sinfulness."

- IV

In the nursery, which was the haven to which they instinctively retreated, the baby slept peacefully under Polly's watchful eye. Ellen waved the girl away and sank trembling into the chair beside the cradle. She was a timid creature, and the recent clash of tempers had left her feeling weak and shaken, horrified by the violence into which her husband's rage had betrayed him. Charity moved across to the fireplace and stood with her back to the room, her hands resting against the beam above the hearth. She had not spoken since Jonas struck her, yet Ellen had the impression that she was neither cowed nor frightened. Rather did her silence suggest a smouldering anger with difficulty held in check.

Sarah, too, was silent until the servant had left them, and then she said in a stricken whisper: "Charity, did you hear what Jonas said to me?"

"Yes, I heard!" Her cousin turned slowly to face her. She was very pale, with a purple-red bruise darkening across one cheek, but her voice was calm and level once more. "It was bound to come soon, Sarah! You are almost seventeen."

"He shall not do it!" Sarah said desperately. "I will not be handed over like so much merchandise to some stranger of my brother's choosing!"

"Do you suppose you will have any choice?" A tinge of bitterness crept into Charity's quiet voice. "Jonas is master here—a fact which he never tires of demonstrating. He will pay no heed to any protests which you may make."

Ellen looked from one to the other in perplexity. "I do not understand!" she complained. "Your brother said only that he would give some thought to the question of your marriage. Why should you shrink from that? It is a woman's rightful destiny, the estate in which the Lord has seen fit to place her."

"Is it?" Sarah said in a breaking voice. "Is that *your* consolation, Ellen, the means by which you resign yourself to being wedded to such a man as Jonas? Well, it will not do for me! I would sooner cast myself into the moat yonder."

She turned and ran from the room, slamming the door behind her. Ellen, shocked and alarmed, was rising to follow when Charity's calm voice detained her.

"Let her be! She has no thought of carrying out that threat."

Ellen sank back again, staring at her in bewilderment. She had observed the close friendship between the two cousins, and now this apparent callousness amazed her. The baby, rudely awakened by the slamming door, began to cry, and Charity picked him up and soothed him as though indifferent to everything but his distress. Ellen watched her for a moment and then shook her head helplessly.

"I do not understand," she said again, "but I think I should go after Sarah and talk to her. Perhaps I could reassure her, soothe these fears which seem to beset her."

Charity's brows lifted, and in the dark eyes below them Ellen saw a flash of mockery. "Is your own marriage so happy, cousin, that you would hold it up to Sarah as an example to be envied?" she said crisply, then seeing Ellen's stricken look, added in a kinder tone: "Oh, forgive me, child! I have no right to speak to you thus, for you have done nothing to merit my anger. I fear I have a sharp temper, and a tongue to match it."

"You have been given good cause for ill humour this day," Ellen replied in a low voice, "and it would be idle to pretend that there is no truth in your words. But you spoke truly also when you told Sarah that she will have no choice in the matter of marriage, and she would do well to learn resignation." She got up and took the baby from Charity, holding him close to her breast and looking down at him with a tender smile. "There is some happiness to be found, after all!"

Charity sat down at the table and rested her head

wearily on her hand. "I had best speak plainly," she said with a sigh. "It is not marriage itself that Sarah fears. She would wed very happily if she might follow her heart in the choice of a bridegroom."

"You mean there *is* a man she desires to wed?" Ellen's tone was shocked, for this was a matter customarily decided, as it had been in her own case, by a young girl's father or guardian.

Charity nodded. "Sarah believes so, but such a match is out of the question. He is a Royalist, Henry Mordisford by name, the brother of Sir Darrell Conyngton's late wife. Sarah met him when he visited Sir Darrell the summer before last." She broke off, frowning, as though her own words brought back memories she did not care to recall.

There was a pause. At last Ellen said in a low voice: "This is all part, is it not, of the mystery I have stumbled upon today? The hatred I sensed in the village, the enmity which so plainly exists between my husband and Sir Darrell."

"Jonas is for Parliament and the Puritan faith," Charity replied with a shrug, "and he is the only man born and bred in these parts who holds such beliefs."

Ellen shook her head. "It is more than that!" she said with conviction. "I know of people in Plymouth who hold fast to your own mistaken loyalties, and they are still regarded as neighbours even though no longer as friends." She paused, looking at Charity with puzzled, unhappy eyes. "*You* must know the truth! You have lived here all your life, and you spoke just now as one who knows the family of Conyngton better than most."

Charity sighed. "Yes, you are right! When we were

children, Darrell and I were as brother and sister, even though he was the squire's son and four years older than I. His parents showed me great kindness, and I loved them dearly. After Darrell was married, I went to Conyngton as waiting-gentlewoman to Alison, his wife, and only returned here when the manor was destroyed. Jonas always resented my friendship with the Conyngtons, the more so since he and Darrell disliked each other." She moved her hands in a little, expressive gesture. "You see, cousin, these differences reach back many years."

"Mere differences do not engender the kind of hatred I sensed in the village this day," Ellen said obstinately. "Charity, in pity's name tell me the truth! What is the secret concerning my husband into which I am not permitted to inquire?"

"It is no secret," Charity replied gravely. "Any man or woman in the village could tell you, but if Jonas has not done so, then he does not desire you to know. Nor is it for me to go against his wishes in this matter." She paused, studying the younger woman's distressed and puzzled face, and her own expression softened. "Let be, child!" she added more gently. "The knowledge could bring you no happiness, and there are some things it were better you do not know."

# 3

THE days lengthened, and with leaf and blossom and the song of birds, spring crept over the land. All her life Charity had taken a passionate delight in the changing seasons, and felt an almost pagan affinity with the rhythms of nature, but this year, for the first time, springtime awoke in her more pain than gladness. The new life burgeoning all about her seemed a cruel mockery, a lovely promise which must remain for ever unfulfilled. When she held Ellen's thriving infant in her arms she thought now not only of a child who had died, but of other children yet unborn, and was filled with vain rebellion against the impatient years.

One breezy, blustery April day she sat spinning in the nursery, with her back resolutely turned to the window beyond which branches bright with new leaves tossed in the sunshine. There was a restlessness within her which the sight of the blossoming world outside could only aggravate. Of late she had found herself thinking more and more often of the possibility of flight, and finding ever greater difficulty in remembering the demands of duty which must prevent it.

So absorbed was she in troubled thought that she

did not hear the approaching footsteps, and when the door opened she looked up with a start. Then she rose hurriedly to her feet, for Ellen, coming into the room, was not alone. A man was with her, a wiry young man with a deeply tanned face, and fair hair bleached almost white by a stronger sun than that of England. His blue eyes were very clear and direct, yet sufficiently like the gentle ones of the girl by his side for Charity to guess before Ellen spoke that he was her kinsman.

"Cousin!" Ellen's voice was breathless with excitement, and she looked happier than Charity had ever seen her. "Here is my brother, Tom, come to visit me! It is nigh a year and a half since last I saw him."

"And until we dropped anchor in the Sound, I did not know that my little sister was wed," Tom Pennan added, smiling affectionately at her. "For the first time, she was not waiting to welcome me home from a voyage."

The words told Charity all she needed to know of the stranger's identity, for Ellen had spoken more than once of her sailor brother. Ellen herself had gone straight to the cradle, but paused in the act of bending over it to add apologetically:

"Your unexpected arrival, Tom, has so overset my wits that I forget my manners. This is Miss Charity Shenfield, my husband's kinswoman."

Charity thought she saw a flicker of surprise in Captain Pennan's eyes as he acknowledged the introduction, but as his attention was immediately claimed again by his sister, she could not be certain. Ellen had picked up little Jonathan and was proudly displaying him, while Charity, standing quietly aside, watched them and wondered with some amusement how Jonas, who was at present away from the house, would react to his brother-in-law. Not very favourably, she suspected. This young sea-captain did not look the sort of man who would be impressed by Jonas Shenfield, nor did it seem likely that Jonas would approve of him. He was dressed without undue extravagance, but his doublet was of a gay crimson, the leather baldrick supporting his sword was buckled in gold, and as he bent over his infant nephew there gleamed through the sun-bleached hair the gold rings he wore in his ears. Altogether he seemed too colorful a figure to fit comfortably into the sober Shenfield household.

That her suspicion was well founded she discovered when the family assembled for supper. Jonas and Tom were being punctiliously civil to each other, but there was already an air of constraint between them. Knowing Jonas so well, Charity guessed that he had made the mistake of patronising Tom Pennan at their first meeting, and such an attitude was not likely to please a man two or three years his senior and accustomed to wielding the unquestioned authority of a ship's captain.

After a while, Ellen asked her brother some question concerning his recent voyage from the New World, and the conversation came round to ships and to those who manned them. Charity, for whom the world beyond the narrow boundaries of her own experience held a constant fascination, hoped that they would now hear some stirring tales of adventure, but to her disgust Jonas said in a minatory tone:

"From my observation of those mariners who frequent the town of Plymouth, madam, I fear that this is no fit subject for your ears, nor for the ears of my mother and sister. I have often deplored the fact that the common seaman is seldom led into the paths of righteousness by the advice and examples of those in authority over him."

Ellen flushed scarlet and subsided in silent confusion, but Tom said equally: "A captain's authority ends with the voyage, and after long months at sea, men cannot be blamed for seeking a trifle of harmless pleasure."

'Harmless pleasure, sir?" Jonas repeated indignantly. "One may see them any day roistering around the town, drinking, swearing and wenching, an offence to men and an abomination in the eyes of the Lord!"

There was an instant's pause and then Tom said, pleasantly enough but with a hint of steel in his level tone: "If the roistering mariners did not dare the hardships and dangers of the ocean, Mr Shenfield, the merchants who sit at home would not grow fat upon the trade they bring."

Jonas's face darkened with anger, and for a few seconds the two men eyed each other in silence, while the women watched with dismay and apprehension. Then, as though both had realised the impropriety of an open quarrel, they curbed their anger and the moment of tension was allowed to pass, though it was plain that the incident would be forgotten by neither.

It was an unpropitious beginning to Captain Pennan's visit, and Charity was scarcely surprised next morning when Ellen came into the nursery with her eyes reddened by weeping, and announced that her brother intended to return to Plymouth that day. Pitying the girl's distress and seeking to comfort her, she said after a moment's thought:

"Perhaps he has business to attend to in Plymouth."

Ellen shook her head, her eyes filling again with tears. "How can that be, when he told me yesterday that he would stay with me for several days? He will only say that it is best that he should go, but I know the reason well enough. He thinks that if he stays, he and my husband will quarrel again, but why does he not think a little of me? I believe he no longer has any fondness for me at all!"

Charity comforted her as best she might, but after a little, when she was calmer and had settled down to nurse the baby, went quietly out of the nursery, determined to speak to Captain Pennan herself. She found him in the garden, staring moodily at the sundial, and having bidden him good morning, came to the point with her customary directness.

"Ellen tells me, sir, that it is your intention to leave the Moat House today." He agreed, and she added calmly: "For her sake, I think you should stay."

Astonishment banished his expression of polite attention. They he frowned, and said with equal bluntness, "Why?"

Her brows lifted. "It should not be necessary, sir, to tell *you* how much the presence here of her favourite brother means to Ellen. Do not deprive her of it so soon!"

For a space Tom Pennan was silent, curiously regarding her. The previous day he had judged her to be a shy and ineffectual creature, her spirit broken by the lowly position she was forced to occupy in her kinsman's household, but he realised now how false that impression had been. Quiet and self-effacing though she chose to appear, Charity Shenfield was a person to be reckoned with.

"Did Ellen send you to ask this of me?" he said at length, and saw a gleam of amusement in the dark eyes which looked so levelly into his own.

"No, Captain Pennan, she did not. I have no doubt that she pleaded with you to stay, but since that proved of no avail she accepts your decision without question, no matter what unhappiness it may cause her."

"But you, Miss Charity, do not?"

She shook her head. "It is not in my nature, sir, so readily to accept defeat. Ellen thinks that your intention to depart signifies lack of affection for her. I do not!"

Again a quick frown creased his brow. "Ellen is mistaken! Nothing could lessen my affection for her."

"So I suppose, sir, and that is why I ask you to remain here." She paused, still holding that direct blue gaze with her own, and then added very deliberately: "You are not, I think, a man whose pride is of greater account to him than a sister's tears."

She saw astonishment in his eyes again, and looked mockingly back at him, waiting for some indignant reply, but all he said was: "I trust not, indeed, madam! If it means so much to Ellen, I will stay willingly." For a moment longer he regarded her gravely, and then added with a sudden, quite chuckle: "But if my temper betrays me into a quarrel with your kinsman the blame, Miss Charity, must lie upon *your* conscience, not on mine!"

II

They returned to the nursery, and when Ellen was informed of her brother's intention to remain at the

Moat House she flung herself into his arms and wept again, this time with joy. He teased her a little to comfort her, but Charity could see that he was disturbed. After a while, when Ellen had dried her eyes, he said more seriously:

"Nell, it is not like you to be so easily moved into tears. Are you so unhappy in your new life that a mere visit from me can mean so much to you?"

"Unhappy?" Ellen freed herself from his arms and turned to bend over the cradle; her voice was determinedly cheerful. "Why, Tom, what a foolish question!"

"Nor is it like you to lie to me!" He took her by the arm and turned her again to face him. "Child, you may speak as freely to me now as you have always done; and so that frankness may be matched with frankness, I will tell you plainly that I felt no pleasure when I learned of the marriage which had been made for you."

She gave a gasp of alarm and looked quickly towards Charity, who was now busy at the spinning-wheel on the far side of the room. Seeing the look, Charity said soothingly:

"You should know by now, Ellen, that *I* am not likely to carry tales to Jonas. It seems to me, however, that your brother chooses a strange way to offer you comfort."

"I am a blunt fellow, Miss Charity," Tom replied curtly. "I say again—and will say it to his face should the need arise—that Jonas Shenfield is not the man *I* would have chosen for my sister's husband."

"Oh, Tom, you also?" It was a cry of despair from Ellen. "Why do so many people hate or despise him? You, and Charity, and the people in the village, even his own sister! In the name of pity, what has he done?"

"So they have not told you?" Tom's voice was quiet, with an undertone of bitterness. "No, I suppose not! In Plymouth, Shenfield is a respected and influential man, and already it has been made plain to me by my father and brothers that my opinion is not welcome."

"But what has he done?" Ellen insisted. "Tom, you have said too much now not to tell me the rest!"

"Captain Pennan!" Charity spoke warningly before Tom could reply. "I counsel you to think well what you do! Rumour speaks with a noisy and distorted tongue, and only those who were present know the truth of what befell. Would you destroy your sister's peace of mind for the sake of some wild tale heard long ago?"

He looked curiously at her, and there was respect in his eyes. "You ask mercy for him, who has shown so little to you?" he said quietly. "The sentiment, madam, does you credit, but believe me, I have a more solid basis than rumour upon which to found my judgement, as I shall prove to you. Tell me, does the name 'Dobworthy' stir any recollection in your mind?"

She stared at him, frowning a little, and then her brow cleared. "A family of that name served the Conyngtons. John Dobworthy fell with his master at the battle of Edgehill."

Tom nodded. "Leaving a son, Jacob, a lad of some thirteen years. The boy's mother was dead, and when his father followed Sir Darrell Conyngton to war, Jacob was left in care of his grandfather, a man who had grown old in the family's service."

"Yes, I remember!" Charity's voice was low, her

eyes clouded by memory. "They left the village soon after the manor was burned."

"And in the course of time, young Jacob sought a livelihood at sea," Tom concluded. "He sailed with me on this last voyage, and since I knew his history I sought him out yesterday before coming here and questioned him concerning certain rumours I had heard. He told me the truth about Jonas Shenfield."

"What *is* the truth?" Ellen broke in urgently, and made a gesture of dissent as Charity tried to intervene. "Cousin, he is my husband! I have a right to know!"

Her brother turned to her again. "Yes, Nell, you have a right to know, although it is a wretched tale and one I would there was no need to tell you." He paused, frowning, and then added abruptly: "In the time you have dwelt here, you must more than once have seen the burned-out ruins of the manor on the hilltop yonder. That destruction, child, was wrought at Jonas Shenfield's command."

Ellen gasped, and turned a horrified, questioning glance towards Charity, but the other woman was apparently intent upon her spinning. After a moment Tom went on:

"During the late wars, as you know, your husband espoused the cause of Parliament while the people of these parts were for the King. Shenfield quarrelled violently on that score with the squire's son, he who is now Sir Darrell Conyngton. They fought, Shenfield was publicly humiliated, and as a result went to live with his mother's family in Plymouth. Later, when Sir Darrell was far away with the Royalist army, he took his revenge. He led a troop of Roundhead soldiers here and plundered and burned the manor. Some even say that he was responsible for the death of Sir Darrell's wife."

"No one can with certainty blame Jonas for that!" Charity spoke quietly, her eyes still intent upon the thread she was spinning. "When his soldiers marched upon the manor, Alison Conyngton was about to be confined. We fled here for safety, and that same day her son was born and Alison died, but she was a delicate creature and even at Conyngton might not have survived the birth."

"The child!" Ellen said in a whisper. "The child you cared for as your own! It was Sir Darrell Conyngton's son?"

Charity bowed her head in assent. "My uncle gave us shelter here and thus I was able to rear the babe. It was the only thing I could do for Darrell—the only thing left for me to do."

Ellen's glance went involuntarily to the cradle where her own bonny babe lay sleeping, and she recognised, with a fresh stab of dismay, the cruelty which had prompted the choice of Charity as the infant's nurse. Somehow that proof of her husband's vindictiveness made the whole tale believable.

She remembered Sir Darrell's bleak, stern face, and the silent, fierce hostility of the villagers, and was overwhelmed by despair. Sinking down on a nearby stool, she covered her face with her hands, while above her bowed head, Charity and Tom looked at each other in silence. Then Charity got up and came to lay her hand on Ellen's shoulder.

"It is a wretched tale, child, as your brother said, but one you had to hear sooner or later, and better from us, who care for you, than from someone whose only concern is to wound."

"How can I bear it?" Ellen lifted a white, despairing face towards her. "How can I live here, and be a loyal and dutiful wife, knowing the infamy of which he is guilty?"

"Because you *are* his wife, Ellen, you must strive for compassion and understanding. A great wrong *was* done, and will be neither forgotten nor forgiven in Conyngton St John, but it was done in time of war, when men's deeds may not be measured by ordinary standards. It is over now, and Conyngton and Shenfield live in peace, though never again in friendship."

For a second or two Ellen was silent, and then she gave a deep sigh and straightened her bowed shoulders. "I will try," she said in a low voice. "Will you both leave me now? I should like to be alone for a little while."

Her companions exchanged glances, and then as though by mutual consent did as she asked. When they looked back from the doorway, she was already on her knees beside the cradle, her head bowed in prayer.

In the dark, narrow passage outside the nursery, Tom Pennan looked at Charity. "I thank you for that," he said quietly, "but did you speak the truth, Miss Charity? Is it indeed over? That is not what I heard in Plymouth."

She met his questioning gaze frankly, realising that for once she could speak without reservation. "It will never be over, sir, while my kinsman lives," she said bitterly, "but what avail to tell your sister that? Already she has a heavy enough cross to bear."

Tom Pennan remained at the Moat House for nearly a week, and Charity came to know and to like him. She had felt kindly towards him even before they met, for Ellen had told her how Tom had been obliged to fight both parental disapproval and the traditions of his stolid, merchant family in order to fulfill his ambition to go to sea. Being herself a rebel by nature, Charity's sympathy had been immediately aroused, and acquaintance with Captain Pennan did nothing to diminish it. He possessed a frankness and a humour all too rarely met with at the Moat House.

That he remained there only for his sister's sake was plain enough. He and Jonas never again came as close to an open quarrel as on that first evening, but there passed between them no more than curt civilities, while Elizabeth Shenfield, who always took her son's part, adopted a frigid manner towards the guest. It was a difficult situation, and one which did nothing to lighten the gloom which of recent years had pervaded the household.

Since the day when Ellen had learned the truth of her husband's quarrel with Darrell Conyngton, she had spent as much time as possible in the nursery, and frequently her brother joined her there. Soon Charity found herself looking forward to the times when she and Ellen could sit, busy with sewing or spinning, while the baby gurgled happily in his cradle and Tom talked of the voyages he had made and the strange lands he had seen. Once, observing her intent face and eager eyes, he said with a laugh:

"I vow, Miss Charity, that if you were a man you would take ship with me when I set sail again."

"If I were a man, sir," she retorted crisply, "I would have gone hence long ago. My father left this house as a lad of seventeen, and never again returned to it."

Tom regarded her curiously. "Your father was Shenfield's uncle, was he not?"

"Yes, but I have been told many times that he was no credit to the family." She spoke in a matter-of-fact tone, with a hint of wry amusement. "He left this neighbourhood under a cloud of scandal, eloped some years later with the daughter of a French nobleman, and contrived to get himself killed in a London tavern four months before I was born."

"In London?" Ellen's tone was puzzled. "I thought, cousin, that you were born at the Moat House."

"Why, so I was! My uncle Jonathan brought my mother here after she was widowed, for her own family had cast her off, and she was almost destitute. I must be grateful that he was charitable enough to provide for me."

Tom looked at her rather hard, sensing the bitterness and resentment beneath the non-committal tone, but before anything more could be said the door opened to reveal the stout figure of Elizabeth. For a second or two she remained standing on the threshold, regarding them with an expression of triumphant disapproval, and then, fixing Charity with a steely glance, she said tartly:

"This is a pretty sight, to be sure! Let me tell you, my girl, that there is plenty of work waiting while you sit idling here. The babe does not need your care while his mother is with him, so get you down to the kitchen and see to it that the lazy wenches there do not neglect their tasks."

She paused, prepared, even hoping for the contemptuous words to strike a spark of defiance from her niece, but none came. Charity folded away her sewing and without a word got up and went obediently out of the nursery, while Mrs Shenfield, disappointed in that respect, cast a darkling glance at her daughter-in-law.

"In this house, Ellen, it is not considered seemly to entertain company in the nursery. Captain Pennan may be your brother, but be good enough to remember that he is also your husband's guest."

On that crushing note she departed, and Ellen, aware of the frown which darkened her brother's face, said diffidently:

"No doubt she is right, Tom! I should have guessed that it would displease her to find you here."

"It will need more than that old harridan's spite to drive me hence," she replied bluntly. "She has made it plain enough that my company is not to *her* liking." He hesitated, and then added abruptly, "Does she always treat Miss Charity as though she were a mere servant?"

Ellen sighed. "I fear so, and it troubles me to see it. She bears all he slights so meekly and with such exemplary patience."

"Meekness and patience?" Tom said reflectively. "I would not have said that these were the most notable aspects of Miss Charity's nature. Have you never looked into her eyes? There is a fiery spirit smouldering beneath that demure resignation."

"Mayhap there is, but what can she do but dissemble it? I think you do not realise, Tom, the difficulties which beset a woman in her situation. This house is her only refuge, and she must do as she is bidden in return for its shelter."

"She might marry!"

"Without a dowry? Her cousin will not provide for her to that extent, and besides, she is already nearly two-and-twenty. No, she has no choice but to remain here and bear as best she may the treatment accorded her."

Captain Pennan did not pursue the matter. For the short time remaining of his visit he saw Charity only at table and at prayers, but before leaving for Plymouth the following day, he made a point of seeking her out. Having taken formal leave of her, he went on:

"I shall come to bid my sister farewell before I sail again, and I shall esteem it a favour, Miss Charity, if you will continue to stand her friend. I am by no means easy on her account."

"I will do all I can, sir, I promise you," she replied frankly, "but you must realise by now that with the best will in the world I can offer her no more than sympathy and kindness."

"Those are the two things, madam, of which I believe her to stand in greatest need, and which in this house she is least likely to find. To know that she will receive them from you lets me leave her with an easier mind."

He bowed and went away, and Charity watched him go with some regret. Tom Pennan, she thought, would make a staunch and fearless friend.

# 4

SOME ten days after Tom's departure, Polly came into
the nursery and slipped a sealed note into Charity's
hand. Its contents were brief, merely asking her to
meet Darrell at the gatehouse next morning on a matter
of urgency. She read it twice and then burned it, wondering uneasily what the summons portended.

Next day, as she approached the gatehouse in the
grey and misty dawn, she saw Darrell coming to meet
her. They embraced, but then, instead of answering
her anxious question, he led her in silence to the
doorway of the small, bare room. On the threshold she
halted in astonishment, for another man was standing
within, a slightly built young man in the gay clothes of
the Cavalier.

"Mr Mordisford!" Charity exclaimed. Her surprise
was tinged with dismay, for this was the man with
whom Sarah fancied herself in love. "What brings you
here?"

"One reason, at least, you should not find it hard to
guess," Henry Mordisford replied wryly. "Do I see
you well, Miss Charity?"

"As well as may be in these evil times, sir! And yourself?"

"The same!" He kissed the hand she put out to him, and then, raising his head, looked at her with an eager question in his eyes. "What of Sarah? Does she remember me still?"

"Without a doubt," Charity answered dryly. "Better, perhaps, if she did not." She saw the dismay in his face, and added with a sigh: "Mr Mordisford, your wooing of Sarah is like to prove as fruitless as Darrell's wooing of me. Therefore I ask myself whether it is wise for you to be here. To see her again will mean but another parting, just when time may have begun to heal the pain of the first."

"My love," Darrell put in quietly, "to see Sarah again is not the only purpose of Hal's visit. That is why I asked you to come here, so that we may acquaint you with what we have in mind."

She turned to him, realising for the first time that there was a note of excitement in his voice, a look in his eyes she had not seen there for many a day. Another pang of uneasiness assailed her, and she looked questioningly at Mordisford. He did not immediately respond, but instead looked frowningly at Darrell. After a moment or two he said:

"I say again, Darrell, that this is no matter to lay before a woman. I pray you, think well what you do."

"I have no secrets from Charity," Darrell replied, and took her hand to draw her closer to his side. "What touches me, touches her also, and I would have it no other way."

Charity's fingers responded to the pressure of his, but she continued to watch Mordisford. A faint inkling of what was to come was forming itself in her mind, a suspicion which was presently confirmed.

"So be it!" Hal said resignedly. "Miss Charity, it must be plain to you that when the Roundheads murdered King Charles, God rest him, two courses lay open to his loyal subjects. They might accept the new order and pray for better times, or they might begin to work actively to restore his son to the throne."

"But how may that be done? Surely there is not one Royalist under arms left in all England?"

"Under arms, no!" he relied eagerly. "Yet Royalists there are in their thousands, loyal at heart in spite of the lip-service which expediency prompts them to pay our present masters. It is these loyal men who must be brought together under able leadership, forged into a weapon which will be strong to support the King when he comes again. Yet this must be done secretly if it is to be done at all."

Her startled glance passed from one man to the other. "So conspiracy is what you intended?"

"What other path at present lies open to us? Already there are Royalist agents at work in England. I have spoken with some of them myself." Hal leaned forward, speaking eagerly, his handsome young face and dark grey eyes alight with enthusiasm. "At Gravesend, near my home in Kent, a riverside tavern was used by them as a meeting-place until a few weeks ago. Then the authorities became suspicious and the place was closed, but though they may shut that door, others remain open. I have learned enough to realise that before we can hope to take up arms again, there is much work to be done to prepare the way."

She looked at him for a moment in silence. Her

hand still rested in Darrell's, and she knew that if she turned to look at him she would see in his eyes the same expression that glowed in Hal Mordisford's. This was, in its way, yet another call to arms, and she must steel herself to meet the challenge of it. When at length she spoke, only the faintest tremor of misgiving sounded in her low voice.

"Why here?"

"Because the West has a staunch tradition of loyalty to the Royal cause, and because I knew that Darrell would be as ready to use every endeavour now as he and his father were seven years ago. There was little for me to do in Kent. My brothers already are in communication with the exiled Court, and will bring our people in when the time is ripe. It seemed to me that I could best serve His Majesty by coming here."

"And I am grateful to you," Darrell broke in. "Charity, do you not understand? This is a chance to serve the King again! The name of Conyngton still carries some weight in these parts, and where I lead, there is a chance that others will follow."

She looked at him with troubled eyes. "Half a dozen families at most," she said bitterly, "and all of them, like yourself, impoverished by war and by the fines and taxes imposed by our enemies. Are these the means by which Cromwell is to be dragged down in defeat?"

"If that were all, Miss Charity, you would be right to doubt us," Hal said quickly, "but there are men like Darrell in every county of England. What we do here will be one small part of a greater conspiracy covering the whole of the West, and that in its turn part of a greater design yet, until the whole kingdom is ready to rise in the name of the King."

"And the Roundheads will permit all this to be done? Or is it to be accomplished without their knowledge?"

"Do not scoff at our purpose, Charity!" Darrell said quietly. "The authorities are constantly vigilant and it would be idle to pretend that what we mean to do is without danger; but do it we must!"

"Yes," she replied sadly, "that I know! You told me, did you not, that though you would promise to inform me of any action you proposed to take, you would not hold aloof from it at my bidding? Nor shall I seek to persuade you. I ask only that you will tread as warily as may be, and remember that in this village there is one whose most fervent wish is to destroy you. It is not only against the authorities that you will need to be on your guard."

"I am not likely to forget it," Darrell said grimly, "but I cannot let any consideration of that nature hold me from my duty."

"No," she said wistfully, half to herself, "and I must not seek to hold you from it either. You have trusted me with this secret and now it is for me to prove that your trust is not misplaced. Now I must go back. Jonas is in Plymouth at present, and his minion, Daniel Stotewood, with him, but even so it is not prudent for me to be too long away."

"Miss Charity, wait!" Hal broke in anxiously. "Tell me how I may contrive to see Sarah." She hesitated, and he added urgently: "I must see her! I have hungered for a sight of her these eighteen months."

Charity sighed. "I suppose if I refuse to aid you, you will endeavour it without my help and so court certain discovery. You must understand, though, that while it is difficult for me to slip away, for her it is wellnigh impossible, for she is much more in my aunt's company than I. I can make no promise, but be in the woods above the brook at sunrise tomorrow and she may be able to come to you there."

"The hope of seeing her is enough," he replied fervently. "You place me eternally in your debt! Tell her that if she comes not tomorrow, I will wait there each morning until she is able to do so."

"Very well, but in the name of pity stay out of sight among the trees and do not show yourself where you may be seen from the meadow. Remember, it is Sarah who will have to bear the punishment if you are discovered."

"I will be circumspect, I promise you, and, Miss Charity, Sarah must know nothing of the matters we have spoken of this morning."

"Do you suppose, sir, that I need to be told that? I love Sarah dearly, but I would place no dependence upon her discretion, in that matter or any other."

II

During the next fortnight Darrell went cautiously to work, sounding out the opinions of his neighbours. They were men whom he had known all his life, and many of them had ridden with him and his father to join the Royal army in the first flush of optimism seven years before, but it was a very different story now. Loyalty burned with undiminished fervour, but defeat in war, and the crippling penalties imposed by the victors, had bred a caution which bordered on timidity. Charity, stealing out to meet him at the manor in the scented coolness of a May morning, found him perplexed and disheartened by the apathy he had encountered.

"I cannot comprehend it," he told her dejectedly. "Here at last is a chance to work again on behalf of the King, yet all I receive are evasions and half-promises. It is not what I thought to find."

"Is there no one, then, willing to join with you?" she asked, and felt secretly ashamed of her own hope that it was so. "Must you abandon the project?"

"Never!" he replied emphatically. "I do not entirely lack support, but there is not the whole-hearted response I hoped for. Too many are willing merely to wait upon events, and though they earnestly desire the King's return, to hope that it will be achieved without their active help."

"Is that so blameworthy, my dear? It is no wonder they are reluctant to risk what little they have upon so rash a gamble."

Darrell, leaning against the trunk of the tree beneath which they stood, lifted his gaze to the blackened walls of Conyngton looming above the fresh green foliage. His face was grim, his eyes sombre.

"Better to risk all thus, than to drag out our days without purpose and without hope. To fail, striving for achievement, than to cling in shameful timidity to the few pitiful remnants our enemies allow us."

She sighed, but did not reply, for she knew the futility or argument. Once again the vain bitterness against Jonas swept over her, for she knew, too, that this attitude of mind in Darrell was exactly what he had set out to achieve. For her, life was hard enough, but in the busy round of duties at the Moat House, in the companionship of Sarah and of Ellen, there was sufficient to occupy her thoughts for almost all her waking hours. Darrell, living at the Dower House alone except for his servants, riding solitary about his diminished estate, had ample time to brood, and the hot-headed proposals of his friend, Hal Mordisford, had fallen upon fertile ground.

"That may be true for you, my love," she said gently after a long pause, "but you cannot compel others to think and act as you do. Perhaps the time for such action is not yet ripe."

"Mayhap, but we have not yet given up hope! We must fare farther afield in search of support, that is all." He cast her a quick glance. "It is my mind to sound out Richard Linslade, your cousin Beth's husband, over by Exeter."

"Sir Richard?" Charity's tone was startled. "Darrell, is that wise? Jonas's own brother-in-law?"

"There is no kindness between them! Linslade fought for the King and his loyalty has never been in doubt. As for Beth, she has not been at the Moat House since before her father died."

"No, and 'tis true there is now little enough contact between the two households, but even so—"

"I knew Richard Linslade well in the old days. He is an able man, and one who might well be of use to us in the business we have in mind." He saw the doubt in her face, and added persuasively: "Little one, we must leave no path untried! Hal must have more than mere assurances of our own loyalty to carry the King."

"To the King? Mr Mordisford goes to France?" This time Charity could not keep the relief from her voice, and Darrell frowned a little as he recognised it.

"We have decided that his going is likely to arouse less suspicion than would my own. He will carry with him an account of what resources we can muster, and of our readiness to serve His Majesty in whatever manner he may command."

"Darrell!" Charity caught him by the arms; there was urgency and alarm in her voice. "You are not rash enough to set such matters down in writing?"

He smiled. "Sweetheart, were I mad enough for that, His Majesty would be well advised to have naught to do with so inept a plotter! Be assured that I will set my hand to no incriminating papers." He paused, and then added abruptly: "The prospect of Hal's departure pleases you, does it not?"

"It relieves my mind," she admitted. "As long as he remains here, he and Sarah will continue to meet, and sooner or later those meetings will be discovered. Darrell, can you not dissuade Mr Mordisford from seeing her again?"

"Could any man dissuade *me* from seeing *you* if an opportunity offered? Hal is well aware of the need for caution, so perhaps you should direct these warnings where they are like to be most needed—at your cousin Sarah! She may take heed of you, and bear herself with more discretion henceforth."

Charity thought this unlikely, but by keeping watch she was able to discover Sarah when next she crept out to an assignation with Hal, and was waiting for her in her bedchamber on her return. Sarah let out a squeak of alarm when she saw her, following it immediately with a gasp of relief.

"Charity! Oh, what a fright you gave me!"

"That was my intention," Charity retorted sharply.

"I thought it might serve to bring you to your senses. In pity's name, child, how long do you suppose these constant comings and goings can continue without arousing suspicion? Why risk punishment for the sake of something which can end only in sadness?"

Sarah perched on the edge of the bed and looked defiantly at her cousin. "Why do you?"

"Dear, can you see no difference between your circumstances and mine? There are some compensations for being poor and of no account, for *I* have no value to Jonas save as a weapon with which to strike at Darrell. You, his sister, will be expected to make a good marriage, of advantage to yourself and to your family."

"Does Jonas think to look higher than a Viscount's son for my husband?"

"The youngest son," Charity reminded her dryly, "of an impoverished Royalist family! Do not deceive yourself, Sarah! You will never be allowed to marry Hal Mordisford."

"It could not be prevented," Sarah said slowly, looking sidelong at Charity beneath her lashes, "if we fled together overseas."

"Sarah!" There was more than exasperation now in Charity's voice. "Mordisford has not suggested such a thing?"

"No," Sarah admitted reluctantly, "I did! At first he laughed at me, and then, when he realised that I was in earnest, he grew angry and told me that it was neither honourable nor practical."

Charity breathed a sigh of relief. She had not really believed that Hal, engaged upon his perilous, self-appointed task, would be foolish enough to involve himself in a runaway marriage, but a man in love might promise all manner of folly under the spell of those blue eyes and pretty, pleading ways. She said shortly:

"Praise be, then he is less foolish than you are!"

Sarah eyed her with some resentment. "You treat me like a silly, empty-headed child!" she said sulkily. "I am a woman grown, and have as much right to love a man as you have."

"In the eyes of the world, no woman has that right until a husband be chosen for her. Love is to be looked for after the marriage ceremony, not before."

"Charity, you of all people, have no right to rebuke me on that score!"

Charity sighed. "No, perhaps not, but remember that Darrell has been the heart of my life since I was six years old, and I know him better than I know any other living soul. We are bound together by so many ties besides those of passionate love. By shared sorrow and shared laughter, by memories reaching back into our childhood. That is the bond between us which Jonas will never be able to break, even though he keep us apart until death. With you and Mordisford it is not so." She came to take the younger girl's hands in her own, speaking very earnestly. "Sarah, I am concerned only to shield you from pain! Believe me, there can be no future together for you, and these secret meetings are bound to be discovered by your brother."

"Jonas does not even know that Hal is in Devon!" Sarah's voice was still defiant, but there was a glimmer of uneasiness in her eyes. "Nor is he likely to learn of it as long as he remains in Plymouth."

"Folly!" Charity said shortly. "You know as well as

I do that Mordisford's presence can be no secret from the villagers—indeed, why should it be? If they know of it, so also does Dr Malperne, and he will have informed Jonas, depend upon it. Now all that is needful is for a whisper of *your* secret comings and goings to reach your brother's ears. You know how these Puritan fanatics see sin in everything, no matter how innocent! Sarah, prove that you have indeed put childishness behind you by being strong now! Do not meet Mordisford again!"

"I cannot meet him again at present," Sarah said disconsolately. "It seems that Sir Darrell has business to attend to in Exeter, and Hal goes with him. When they return . . ." She paused for a moment, but then sighed and shook her head. "Oh, Charity, what use to make you a promise I know I shall not be able to keep?"

III

By the end of May, Jonas was home again from Plymouth, to his mother's satisfaction and the dismay of his wife, sister and cousin. Ellen in particular seemed cast down by his arrival. She had always been timid in her bearings towards him, though this was natural enough in a young wife, but now she seemed to shrink from his mere presence. Charity, observing this and knowing that such a reaction would bring out the very worst in Jonas's nature, regretted bitterly that Ellen had discovered, through the story of the wrongs he had done Darrell, the ugly truth about him. She blamed herself, even though she knew that such a discovery would have had to come some day, and as she saw his manner towards his wife become increasingly harsh, was hard put to it not to take him to task over it.

The very evening of his return gave them ominous warning of his temper. They had finished supper, a gloomy meal overshadowed by Jonas's presence, and by his endless discourse, interrupted only by admiring comments and questions from Elizabeth, upon his own importance and growing influence in Plymouth. The servants had left them, and Charity was waiting with concealed impatience for permission to withdraw, feeling glad that her lowly position in the household excluded her from family evenings in the parlour.

Jonas swallowed the last of his wine, leaned back in his chair and looked deliberately at each of his companions in turn. "Daniel Stotewood informs me," he said heavily, "that Henry Mordisford is at the Dower House."

There was a pause. Sarah sat as though petrified, not daring to look at her brother, while Ellen flushed scarlet and looked as guilty as though she, and not Sarah, had been stealing out to secret assignations with Hal. Only Charity succeeded in appearing unmoved.

"Your spy wastes no time, cousin," she replied boldly, "since he only returned with you from Plymouth this day! Is it so remarkable that Mr Mordisford should visit Darrell? They are kin, and very close friends."

"So they are, to be sure!" There was harsh mockery now in Jonas's voice. "Malignants both, very close in each other's counsels, and now, so Stotewood has discovered, both are absent upon some mysterious business in Exeter. When such as they consort together, honest men had best beware."

A sudden, sick dismay took Charity by the throat. She had at first supposed the reference to Hal to be an indication that Jonas had discovered his wooing of Sarah, but this was worse, far worse. It might be no more than a malicious gibe at two known Royalists who had acquitted themselves in the wars with a distinction which Jonas himself envied but could not emulate, and yet it came perilously close to the truth. Somehow his thoughts must be diverted from their dangerous course.

"Then you may rest easily, Jonas," she said distinctly, "for what do you know of the ways of honest men?"

There was a concerted gasp from the other women, of outrage from Mrs Shenfield, and dismay from Ellen and Sarah. Jonas's eyes narrowed. He thrust back his chair and got up to walk round the table until he stood behind Charity's chair.

"You grow reckless, cousin," he said with a sneer, "and show us a glimpse of that intransigent temper and undutiful spirit which of late you have been learning to hide. Have you so soon forgotten what punishment I promised you if you defied me again?"

She leaned back to look up at him over her shoulder, her dark eyes glinting wickedly. "Dear coz," she replied with dulcet mockery, "how could I ever forget anything you say to me?"

The dark flush which always betrayed his rising temper showed dangerously in his cheeks, and his hand came down heavily upon her shoulder. "This you will certainly not forget," he said savagely, "for I will give you good cause to remember it. A lesson which you will bear upon your body for many a day to come."

Charity shrugged, feigning an indifference she did

not feel. She knew, only too well, the extremes of violence to which Jonas could go under the goad of the almost insane anger which sometimes possessed him, and a wave of sick terror passed over her as she realised what might now await her at his hands. As though reading her thoughts, he laughed without mirth.

"This time, mistress, you have over-reached yourself! Darrell Conyngton is not at hand to come to your aid."

"No, he is not!" She seized swiftly upon the only thing which might thwart his anger before it became ungovernable. "But remember, Jonas, that when he returns there will be a reckoning to pay."

"Then it is not I who will pay it! Have I not waited for years for Conyngton to be provoked into casting caution aside and committing some folly which will encompass his ruin? Now you, cousin, have delivered him into my hands!"

She saw with dismay the trap into which she had fallen. In her anxiety to divert Jonas's mind from any suspicion of the conspiracy she had gone too far, giving him the excuse for punishment which hitherto she had been so careful to avoid. Her heart sank, but she made a last effort to retrieve her mistake by playing upon his lack of physical courage.

"Cold comfort, Jonas, if he kill you first," she said boldly, "and that he will do, cost him what it may, if I suffer any hurt at your hands."

Jonas's grip shifted from her shoulder to her arm, and he jerked her roughly to her feet. Across the table she caught a glimpse of Mrs Shenfield watching her with malicious satisfaction, and next to her, Sarah's horrified face. Then Jonas swung her round to face him, and though his face was still dark with anger, she read a suspicious question in his eyes.

"There is something here which I do not understand," he said abruptly. "What devious purpose, mistress, do you seek to serve by baiting me? You are not fool enough to provoke without good reason such punishment as I shall inflict upon you." He paused, but she made no reply. Jonas laughed. "Stubborn as ever, eh? No matter! I will have the truth from you before all is done."

"Jonas, wait!" Sarah's voice was breathless and unsteady. She pushed back her chair and got up to come round the table towards them. "I beg you not to punish Charity! I will answer your question though she will not."

"Sarah!" Charity said sharply. "There is no need for this!"

"There is every need. I will not let you suffer on my account." Sarah turned again to her brother. She was deathly pale, but faced him with attempted boldness. "Mr. Mordisford came to Devon to see me, Jonas! That is what Charity has been trying to conceal from you."

"To . . . see . . . you?" Jonas repeated slowly. He let Charity go, and stood staring at his sister as though seeing her for the first time. "I think you mock me, Sarah! Or am I expected to believe this story?"

"You may believe it, Jonas, for it is the truth. We love one another, and wish to marry."

He continued to stare at her, and then slowly anger began to conquer stupefaction and he swung abruptly to face their mother.

"You hear, madam? Is this how you rear your daughter in modesty and filial duty, that she may shame herself and offend our ears with such lewd talk?" He gave Elizabeth no chance to reply, but turned savagely on Sarah again. "To what lengths has this affair gone? Is he your lover?"

"No!" Color flamed into Sarah's white cheeks. "He seeks my hand in honourable marriage, and would have come to ask it of you had there been the least hope that you would consent."

"Is this the truth?" He gripped her by the shoulders, thrusting his face close to hers. "Answer me honestly, girl, in fear of the Lord and in the hope of salvation! Are you still virtuous?"

"Yes," she replied furiously, "I am, and in asking such question, Jonas, you shame yourself more than you shame me!"

"That is not for you to judge!" He loosed his hold on her, thrusting her contemptuously away from him so that she staggered back against the table. "Well for you that you can answer me so, but mark this, Sarah! Whom you wed, and when, and all else pertaining to the marriage, is for me to decide, and my choice will not fall upon Henry Mordisford! And if it come to my knowledge that you have met with him again, or communed with him in any way, then 'tis you will suffer punishment, not Charity. Ellen!" He turned abruptly to his wife, who gave a start and a gasp of alarm. "Take my sister to her bedchamber, lock the door and bring the key to me. Perhaps solitude and reflection may bring her to a more proper frame of mind."

Ellen got up hurriedly, only too eager to escape, but Sarah hung back, looking anxiously from her brother to Charity, who still stood by the table, feigning a composure she did not really feel. Jonas, too, turned a boding glance upon his cousin, but Sarah's intervention had given him time to reflect upon the truth of her warning concerning Darrell. His hatred of the other man had always been partly rooted in fear of him.

"Go back to the nursery," he commanded roughly, "and since it seems that both you and Sarah have ample leisure for mischief, my mother shall see to it that additional tasks are found to occupy your time henceforth."

He waved them irritably away, and when the door had closed behind them, returned to his seat at the head of the table and filled his glass again.

"To be burdened with a pack of foolish, disobedient women is a sore affliction," he said aggrievedly, "and you, madam, would do well to discipline them with a firmer hand!"

"Sarah *must* be married soon," Elizabeth replied shortly. "I have advised this, my son, as well you know, but you said merely that you had not yet found a match for her sufficiently advantageous to yourself. You must curb your ambition in that respect, it seems!"

He brushed this impatiently aside. "Sarah's future can be settled at any time that so pleases me. There is no difficulty there. It is the other pert wench who is a constant thorn in my flesh, defying me in my own house from the shelter of Conyngton's damned protection! Would that I could discover a way to rid myself of them both!"

# 5

SARAH's confession concerning Hal Mordisford brought
upon her no worse punishment than a few days' confinement to her room, a number of the most dreary tasks
her mother could devise, and a long lecture from her
brother on the wickedness and folly of her conduct. She
was thankful to escape so lightly, but Charity found
Jonas's forbearance sinister and wondered uneasily
what would happen when Hal and Darrell returned
from Exeter.

Their absence seemed to her to be unduly prolonged,
and though she realised that negotiations so delicate
could not be hurried, and dreaded what might happen
when they came back, the longer they were away, the
more anxious she grew. Nor was the waiting made any
easier by Sarah, who, desperate now for Hal's return,
plagued her with questions concerning the nature of
the business which had necessitated the journey. Charity placated her as best she might, and tried to disguise
her own anxiety as the summer days went by and no
word came.

Early in June, Ellen's spirits were further cast down
by a visit from her brother, who came, as he had

promised, to bid her farewell, his ship being ready to put to sea again. He stayed only one night at the Moat House, and Charity saw that in his presence Ellen was making a brave attempt to pretend that all was well between her and Jonas. Charity did not think it likely that Captain Pennan would be deceived.

She had no chance that evening to exchange more than ordinary civilities with him, but next day, just before his departure, he came with his sister to the nursery. While Ellen was preoccupied with the baby, Charity took the opportunity to ask Tom what news was current in Plymouth, for since Darrell had been away she had heard nothing but such vague rumours as circulated among the servants. Tom looked at her in some surprise.

"But Shenfield has only recently returned from Plymouth, Miss Charity! It is unlikely that I can add anything to the news he must surely have brought."

She shook her head. "My kinsman, sir, is of the opinion that women should concern themselves only with domestic matters, and since we are isolated here, cut off even from the gossip of the village, I have no means of knowing what is passing in the world. Tell me, I pray you, *any* tidings of moment which you may have heard."

He was silent for a moment, thoughtfully regarding her, and then he said slowly: "Well, madam, it is said that Cromwell is for Ireland with the larger part of the Army, to wage war against the papists there and so divert his soldiers from the dissensions which now occupy them. There are rumours of Royalist plots, and I have heard that some arrests have been made."

Charity's heart seemed to stop beating for a fraction of time, and it was only with a tremendous effort that she kept her voice steady enough to say: "Royalist plotters in Plymouth, sir? Surely not!"

"No, not in Plymouth! It is in the south-eastern counties that the alarm has been raised and the supposed plotters seized, though how much truth is in the story I know not. There will be many such tales abroad, no doubt, now that conspiracy is the only means by which Royalists can hope to serve the King."

She looked sharply at him, her black brows drawing together in a frown. "You say 'Royalists', sir, and 'the King'. In this house it is customary to speak of 'malignants' and 'Charles Stuart'."

He returned the look quizzically. "Yet I would be willing to wager, Miss Charity, that *you* do not speak so."

"*I* do not, most certainly, but my loyalties are sadly out of tune with those of the rest of the household. The same blood does not necessarily mean the same opinions."

"That is true, Miss Charity, of other families besides your own. To me, the King is still the King, exiled though he be—and although my father and brothers are staunch supporters of Parliament."

"Would it not be more prudent, Captain Pennan, for that truth to remain unspoken?" she asked curiously, and saw the glimmer of a rueful smile in his eyes.

"More prudent by far, but I knew before I uttered it that no one who has been as close as yourself to the family of Conyngton could be anything but true to the King, so the risk was none so great." He paused to glance quickly at his sister on the far side of the room, and then added quietly, and very seriously, "I would not have you think of me as an enemy, Miss Charity, but as a friend, to be called upon at need for any help which may lie within my power to give."

There was no time to say more, for Ellen came across to them with the baby in her arms, and Charity, knowing how distressed she was by her brother's imminent departure, went quietly away and left them together, merely bidding Tom farewell and wishing him God-speed on his voyage. He had given her a good deal to think about, not least his surprising declaration of Royalist sympathies, for it had never occurred to her that a member of the family from which Jonas had chosen his bride could be anything but a staunch Parliamentarian.

His parting words puzzled her a little, and she wondered for a few uneasy minutes whether he could possibly have any suspicion of Darrell's seditious activities, but at length she decided that this could not be so. His offer of help was no more than a friendly gesture from one who recognised her uncomfortable circumstances, and who was grateful for the sympathy she had given his sister.

II

The anxious days dragged by, and at last, on a hot, still evening when the scent of new-mown hay hung sweetly in the air, Polly brought word that Darrell was home at last and would be waiting at Conyngton the next morning. Thereafter the short summer night seemed endless to Charity, and the dawn was still grey as she went hurrying across the meadow and up the wooded hillside beyond.

As she came in sight of the park she saw that Darrell, with an impatience as consuming as her own, had not waited at the manor but was coming instead to meet her. They met just beyond the edge of the wood, joy at their reunion so great that it overwhelmed for a time every other thought and feeling, so that they were unaware of the rustling in the undergrowth, or of the shadow which moved furtively from tree to tree towards them.

It was Darrell who first became conscious of it. He lifted his head sharply to stare towards the wood, and then, almost before Charity realised what was happening, he had put her aside and moved swiftly forward to vanish behind the broad trunk of the nearest tree. There was a brief scuffle, a fierce imprecation abruptly stifled, and then he appeared again dragging Daniel Stotewood with him by the scruff of his neck. He hauled his captive into the open and then released him with a shove which sent him sprawling on hands and knees at Charity's feet.

"Crawl there in the dirt, where you belong!" Darrell said savagely. "Your master goes too far, sirrah, when he sends you to spy upon me in my own domain."

Stotewood scrambled to his feet, his gaunt face livid with fury, and Charity, looking at him, was suddenly assailed by fear, for in that instant she knew that Daniel Stotewood hated both her and Darrell as bitterly as, and perhaps more dangerously than did Jonas himself. Jonas's hatred was a worldly thing born of jealousy and greed and injured pride, but Stotewood was a religious fanatic whose mind had been warped by the harsh doctrines of the Puritan faith. He glared at her, his pale eyes blazing wildly, and said in a tone of harsh accusation:

"My master has turned away his eyes from the Lord, and his feet from the paths of godliness! He chastiseth not the woman of sin, but allows her to dwell in his house and consort with the righteous!"

Charity started forward and clutched Darrell by the arm, fearing, from the expression in his face, that he was about to do the serving-man some violence. Clinging to him with both hands, she said urgently:

"Let him be, Darrell! He is not worthy of your wrath!"

With a visible effort Darrell mastered the anger which possessed him, and said curtly to Stotewood: "If you value your safety, fellow, get you gone, and do not venture upon my land again. I am not yet brought to so sorry a state that I must suffer without protest the insolence of an upstart lackey!"

Stotewood started to speak again, but Darrell, in spite of Charity's restraining hands, took a threatening pace towards him, and something in his face gave a warning which penetrated even Stotewood's fervour of righteousness. He beat a hasty and undignified retreat, but halted just within the wood and raised his hand in a gesture which was at once wild and menacing. Then he turned and vanished from their sight, and they heard him go crashing blindly down the narrow, overgrown path towards the stream.

Charity leaned weakly against Darrell, her forehead against his shoulder, for she was trembling from head to foot. He held her gently and murmured loving reassurance, troubled to see her so distressed. Charity's spirit, her courage in the face of danger, were so well known to him that her reaction to the brief, violent encounter with Stotewood filled him with dismay.

"There is nothing to fear, my heart's dearest," he said gently. "Yonder was naught but an evil-minded rogue creeping to do his master's unsavoury work!"

"Jonas did not send him!" Charity lifted a white face towards him; her voice held a note of complete conviction. "I am certain that *he* seeks no closer knowledge of our meetings. Stotewood followed me this morning on his own account. He watches me constantly, and upbraids me for my fancied sins whenever the opportunity offers."

"Damnation upon his impudence!" Anger and frustration throbbed in Darrell's low voice. "Had I known that, he would not have escaped so lightly. And Jonas, no doubt, is well pleased to have him berate you so!"

"No doubt, if he is aware of it!" Her fright was passing now, and she spoke in something approaching her normal tone. "'Tis my belief that Jonas himself begins to weary of a servant who regards himself as the keeper of his master's conscience." She paused, studying his disturbed and angry face, and forced herself to smile. "My love, let us put the fellow from our minds! He alarmed me for a moment, but that is a folly of which I am already ashamed. Tell me how you fared in Exeter."

He looked narrowly at her, but she bore the searching regard with a tranquillity which seemed to satisfy him, for he nodded. "I will tell you, but let us walk on into the open park. Doubtless there is little fear of being overheard at present, but we shall do well to cultivate a habit of vigilance." They began to stroll towards the manor, his arm about her shoulders, and he went on: "Our business took longer than we expected, for these are matters which cannot be hurried. It is not possible to ride up to a man's door and ask him outright if he will serve his King in ways which will mean ruin and imprisonment if they become known."

"You approached Sir Richard Linslade?"

"Yes, and found him apt to the business. He contrived to draw in two of his neighbours also, so our errand was by no means without profit."

"How fares Mr Mordisford? He returned with you, did he not?"

Darrell shook his head. "No, it was decided that we have gone as far as may be at present, and that the time had come to acquaint His Majesty with our readiness to serve him. Hal is already on his way to France." He saw the expression in her face, and frowned a little. "That pleases you, does it not?"

"It relieves my mind, Darrell, more than I can say. Jonas knows now how matters stand between Mr Mordisford and Sarah."

Briefly she recounted the manner in which he had learned of it, and Darrell's face grew grim as he listened. He caught her in his arms again, holding her in a hard embrace.

"It is wrong that you should stand in danger of violence at his hands, and I be helpless to protect you! God help us! To what pass are matters come when I cannot even guard that which is dearest to me!"

"Hush, my dear! Your protection is about me always, for not even Sarah's confession would have saved me had Jonas not known that for anything inflicted

87

upon me he must answer to you. It was that alone which stayed his hand."

"Time was when even to threaten such an outrage was more than he would have dared," Darrell said bitterly. "You must promise me never to risk such danger again, no matter how urgent the cause."

"How can I make such a promise," she protested, "when we cannot tell what peril may threaten you, and the Cause we both seek to serve? I will promise, though, never again to provoke Jonas in that fashion save in the last extremity. Now put that from your mind, and tell me instead how I am to account to Sarah for Mr Mordisford's failure to return. She has plagued me sorely with questions as it is."

"You will have to tell her that he has been summoned home to Kent on some family business which brooks no delay. That, in fact, is the reason he gives in this letter he has sent her." Charity looked dubiously at the sealed letter which he had produced, and, seeing her expression, he nodded.

"I know what you are thinking," he said resignedly, "for I, too, doubt the wisdom of it, but Hal was so insistent that I could not bring myself to refuse. This is no trifling matter to him, Charity, no idle dalliance. I believe that if he cannot have Sarah, he will never marry."

"Then he is like to go unwed to his grave, for Jonas will never give consent," Charity replied crossly, but she took the letter and put it into the pocket of her gown. "I suppose if you have promised Mr Mordisford that the letter will reach Sarah, reach her it must, but rest assured that I will make her destroy it as soon as she has read what it contains."

"That will be the most prudent course," he agreed. "I told Hal that no secret matter, whether of the heart or aught else, should be set down in writing, but he would pay no heed. God grant he prove more discreet a conspirator than he is a lover!"

## III

Sarah's disappointment that Hal had not returned was bitter and profound, but since she was an inveterate optimist she was able after a while to convince herself that it was better so. If he had come back with Darrell a crisis would almost certainly have been provoked, and with Jonas in his present mood there could have been little hope of a happy outcome. An interval would give her brother's suspicions time to subside, and by the time Hal came again to Devon some solution to the problem might have suggested itself. Charity, being taken into her confidence, could not agree, but a second attempt to persuade Sarah to renounce her ill-starred love affair met with no more success than the first.

Throughout the rest of June and the first part of July, life at the Moat House followed its accustomed course. Then some matter of business took Jonas again to Plymouth, and when he returned he brought a guest with him, which was an occurrence unusual enough to send a ripple of curiosity through the entire household.

Edward Taynton was a good deal older than Jonas, a grave-faced, somewhat taciturn man in his late thirties. Charity, encountering him for the first time at the dinnertable on the day of his arrival, observed that both her cousin and her aunt were exerting themselves to be agreeable to him, and wondered idly what his claim to importance might be. Later, in the nursery, she asked Ellen if she knew anything about him.

"Mr Taynton?" Ellen repeated in surprise. "Why cousin, there is little that I can tell you! Before my marriage I saw him sometimes at my father's house, but what business brought him there I do not know."

"If he is your father's friend, you must know something about him," Charity said impatiently. "Is he a merchant? A soldier? A scholar?"

"A merchant, I suppose, though I have heard it said that he bore arms with honour during the late wars. He must be rich, for he has a very fine house in Plymouth. His widowed sister keeps it for him, for his wife died some years ago and though he has numerous daughters, the eldest can even now be no more than fourteen years old."

"That he is rich I guessed," Charity remarked with a touch of scorn, "for Jonas does not concern himself with those who are not. No doubt he expects Mr Taynton to be of use to him, since he is at such pains to flatter him."

"Very likely, for I have just remembered something else!" Ellen, dandling little Jonathan on her knee, looked up with an air of triumph. "Mr Taynton has a younger brother who won great honour during the wars, and is now a person of importance in London. Rumour even has it that he is close to General Cromwell himself."

"Now we come to the truth, it seems!" The contempt had deepened in Charity's voice. "A rich man with a brother in high places! No wonder Jonas is exerting himself to please."

Mr Taynton stayed at the Moat House for three days, and then departed leaving Charity no wiser than before but decidedly uneasy. Ellen's talk of a brother in Cromwell's service had an ominous sound, and she wondered anxiously whether this could be the beginning of some obscure move against Darrell, though even if it were it seemed to offer no explanation of Taynton's visit. While it lasted he had not once, to her knowledge, left the immediate surroundings of the Moat House.

An explanation was soon to be forthcoming. That same evening she was busy in the nursery when Ellen burst into the room, white-faced and distracted, gasping out disjointed phrases which at first seemed to make little sense.

"Charity, go down to the parlour! She must be mad to defy him so! Oh, why did we not guess what was in his mind? He will do her some mischief—beside himself with anger, and her mother also! Oh, for pity's sake, make haste!"

She dropped into a chair, gasping for breath, but waving Charity away when she went to her in concern.

"I am well enough! 'Tis Sarah! Go down—she may take heed of you!"

For a second or two Charity stared at her, frowning, and then she turned and ran from the room, along the passages and down the stairs to the hall. A knot of servants, whispering together, clustered around the closed door of the parlour, from beyond which came the sound of voices raised in furious anger. Charity thrust past the group without a glance. She still did not know what had sparked off this explosion, but Ellen's urgency had convinced her that there was no time to be wasted.

When she entered the room her aunt was seated in her usual chair beside the fireplace, her hands gripped hard upon the arms, her stout figure and set face rigid with exasperation. Jonas stood with his back to the empty hearth, feet wide-planted, hands on hips, face dark with fury as he glared at his sister. Sarah herself was standing in the middle of the room. Her back was towards the door, and as Charity entered she was saying in a high, defiant tone:

". . . never do it! You cannot force me to agree to so loathsome a thing!"

"You will do as I bid you!" Her brother's voice shook with the intensity of his rage. "It is not a matter for you to decide!" His scowling glance alighted on Charity, and his next words were addressed to her. "So *you* are here, are you? Methought it would not be long before you came thrusting and prying into what is no concern of yours!"

"Charity!" Sarah spun round, and then flung herself into her cousin's arms. "Oh, Charity, what am I to do? Jonas wants me to marry that old man!"

Charity clasped her in a reassuring embrace, though she was still somewhat at a loss. Then Mrs Shenfield said sharply:

"May God forgive you, Sarah, for such pertness and disrespect! Mr Taynton is *not* an old man, and only a silly wilful child would so describe him."

"He is old enough to be my father!" Sarah retorted tearfully. "He has a daughter not many years younger than I! I heard him tell you so!"

Understanding broke suddenly through Charity's bewilderment, and she wondered why she had not guessed Jonas's purpose before. If he did see Edward Taynton as a useful stepping-stone to the furtherance of his own ambitions, what better way to bind the man to his interest than by marriage to his sister? What better way to set her beyond Hal Mordisford's reach?

"It is not a question, Sarah, of what I want, but of what I intend!" Jonas's voice broke harshly into her hurrying thoughts. "The marriage was agreed upon between Taynton and myself before he left this house."

"After he had inspected me and found me to his liking!" Anger and bitterness throbbed in Sarah's voice. "That is why he came here, was it not? That I might be paraded before him like some beast of burden he might wish to purchase!"

Mrs Shenfield uttered an exclamation of outrage and despair. "Hark to the wench! Never did I think to hear a daughter of mine utter words so wickedly defiant! You were wise, my son, to wait until Mr Taynton had departed before telling her that she is to marry him."

"I knew well enough what kind of outcry she would make," he agreed sourly. "She has been led into this disobedience and folly by evil companions, and had I shown real wisdom her defiance would have been crushed by severe punishment at its very outset, two years since. I was lenient, and now reap the harvest of my own weakness, though you may be sure, madam, that I shall be weak no more."

"Your weakness, my son, has not been so much towards your sister as towards the one who has fostered this sinfulness in her," Elizabeth retorted, looking

93

malevolently at Charity. "There lies the true source of the evil!"

"Do I not know it?" Jonas strode forward until he was close to Charity, where she stood with Sarah sobbing in her arms. "This is your doing, cousin, the fruit of your wanton and deceitful counsels."

"That is absurd, Jonas, and you know it!" she retorted fearlessly. 'But even if it were, 'tis scarcely seemly that you should speak of it so loudly while half your household wags curious ears outside the door."

"What?" He stared at her for an instant, taken aback by this swift counter-attack, and then strode past her to fling open the door. The loitering servants, unprepared for his abrupt appearance, scattered in confusion and were sped on their way by sundry threats of punishment. When they had gone, he closed the door and turned again to the two young women, but the diversion, it seemed, had dulled the edge of his rage.

"I desire to hear no more of this," he informed them. "I have told you, Sarah, of the manner in which I have made provisions for your future, and I will listen to no more protests. Edward Taynton is a sober and godly man, and one of the foremost citizens of Plymouth. It is an excellent match and I will permit nothing to stand in the way of it, least of all this sickly, contemptible fancy you feel towards Henry Mordisford."

Sarah lifted her head from Charity's shoulder and looked at her brother. Tears filled her eyes and trickled down her cheeks, but she spoke calmly, although in a trembling voice.

"I will not marry him, Jonas! You may threaten me as much as you like, punish me as you please, but I will not do it. You would have to drag me by force to such a marriage ceremony, and even if you did that I would still refuse to speak the vows. That I swear to you!"

# 6

To THIS determination Sarah held fast, repeating it later to Charity and to Ellen. The latter, shocked and dismayed, advised her urgently to put all thought of Mr Mordisford from her mind and resign herself instead to becoming the wife of Edward Taynton. Jonas, said Ellen, would find some means of prevailing, and since this was so certain, what was to be gained by fighting against the inevitable? Sarah scorned such craven counsels, and secretly begged Charity to see that word of her plight was sent to Hal. Charity, knowing this to be impossible, prevaricated for as long as she could, and, when finally obliged to agree, warned Sarah that even if such news reached him there was little that Hal could do.

"He can come here and take me away with him to France or Holland," Sarah retorted confidently, "and he will do so, make no doubt of that! He will never allow me to be forced into marriage with another man."

From this conviction nothing could shake her, and at last Charity abandoned all attempts to do so. Privately, she agreed with Ellen that Jonas would prevail in the end, and this opinion seemed to be borne out by his own attitude. There were no more scenes such as that which had greeted his first announcement of the proposed marriage. Having issued his commands he did not repeat them, but he made no secret of the fact he and Taynton, and their respective lawyers, were engaged in drawing up the marriage contract.

At the Moat House, Elizabeth Shenfield had the domestic preparations equally well in hand. Puritan belief frowned upon both the religious significance of the wedding ceremony and the colourful celebrations which in the past had always followed it. There would be no feasting and dancing, no vying for bride-favours at Sarah's wedding as there had been when her sister Beth was married just before the Civil War. At that time their father had been alive and their brother's conversion to the Puritan faith a matter for contempt or laughter.

None the less, there were many preparations to be made, and Elizabeth and her maids, Ellen, Charity and even the reluctant bride herself were kept more than usually busy. Sarah was given little opportunity for open defiance. If she repeated her determination to resist the marriage by every means in her power, Jonas and his mother, apparently by mutual consent, paid not the smallest heed, and this cut the ground from beneath her feet in a way no anger or severe punishment could have done.

So as the summer waned, life in the parish of Conyngton St John continued with apparent uneventfulness, though beneath that placid surface secret currents were stirring. The villagers were staunchly loyal to their squire, and if he was now from home more frequently than at any time since his return from the wars two years before, and had at last begun to entertain guests at the Dower House, these were not matters about which they saw fit to gossip. To do so might attract the attention of Dr Malperne, and thus of the hated master of the Moat House.

The harvest ripened and was gathered in; the first frosts touched the green woods with bronze and gold, and as autumn laid its misty veil across the countryside Sarah's brave certainty began to falter a little. There had been no word from Hal. Charity, who had been obliged to let her think that the news had been sent to him, tried to soften the blow by pointing out how easily, in those uncertain times, a letter could go astray, and tried once more to reconcile her to a marriage which everyone but she regarded as inevitable. She loved Sarah, and her heart ached for her distress, but there were matters of graver and more perilous import to be considered. Charity would have sacrificed anyone, herself included, to keep from Jonas any whisper of the conspiracy in which Darrell was now engaged.

In October the banns of marriage between Edward Taynton and Sarah Shenfield were called for the first time in the little parish church of St John, and Sarah hid her rising panic behind a mask of meek resignation. She was still prepared to resist her brother's determination to the uttermost limit, but she would not abandon hope of rescue by Hal until the wedding day itself. A week went by, the banns were read a second time, and still no sign of deliverance offered itself. Charity, watching her and guessing her agony of mind, was filled with a helpless compassion she would not allow herself to show.

Another week passed with a sense of unspoken,

mounting tension for Jonas had let it be known that when the banns had been published for the third time, the wedding itself would almost immediately follow. Thanks to the servants who had overheard the quarrel between brother and sister, the whole household was aware of the situation, and from the house, that knowledge had passed to the outdoor servants and thence through the entire village, so that everyone was wondering whether Sarah would make good her threat to carry defiance of her brother even to physical lengths. For the most part, sympathy was on her side, as it would be for anyone who suffered at Jonas Shenfield's hands.

On the Saturday of that week, midway through the afternoon, Charity was in the nursery when Sarah came bursting into the room. Charity stared, for her cousin's cheeks were flushed and her eyes shone with a light which had been absent from them for months. She flung herself upon Charity and hugged her.

"Oh, dear coz, you were wrong! Heaven be praised, you were wrong! I knew he would not fail me!"

Sudden dismay took Charity in its grip. She caught Sarah by the arms, freeing herself from her clasp and then holding her before her. "Sarah, what mean you? What has happened?"

"Hal is here, in the village!" Sarah's voice dropped to a breathless whisper; her eyes were like stars. "William has just returned from there. He was at the forge, and he saw Hal and a servant ride by on their way to the Dower House. As soon as he got back, he found an opportunity to tell me."

William was the head groom, a middle-aged man who had been in the family service all his life. Sarah, the youngest, had always been his favourite among the children, and Charity could imagine the delight with which he had brought home his news.

"I knew that he would come!" Sarah's voice, trembling between tears and laughter, broke in upon her thoughts. "I knew it, and yet time was growing so short! But he is here now, and all will be well."

The baby, disturbed by her noisy entry, had begun to cry and Charity went to soothe him, glad of an excuse to hide her face from Sarah. It must, she thought, betray the disquiet she felt. Only pure chance could have brought Hal Mordisford to Conyngton St John that day, and since he could know nothing of Sarah's imminent marriage, he must have come upon the King's business. She could foresee endless complications, all threatening disaster to the conspiracy and danger to the one she loved best in all the world.

Sarah's next words confirmed these forebodings. Coming to stand at Charity's side, she said softly: "As soon as everyone has gone to bed, I shall slip out and go to the Dower House. No one will know of my departure until morning, and thus we shall be a few precious hours ahead of any pursuit. I suppose that for your own sake I should not tell you this, but I could not go without bidding you farewell."

"Sarah, have you lost your wits?" Charity swung round to face her, the baby in her arms. "Do you imagine that you could walk out of this house unhindered and elope with Hal Mordisford when no plans have been made, no preparations for flight?"

"Hal will have laid his plans, depend upon it!" Sarah said confidently. "Why else should he have tarried so long in coming, if not for that purpose?"

Unable to answer this question truthfully, Charity countered it with another. "Have you paused to think what would follow so mad a flight? Even if you won free, you would be obliged to go into exile, to live among strangers far away from friends and kinfolk, and if any harm befell Mordisford you would find yourself alone and poor in a foreign land."

"If I remain here, I shall find myself married to Mr Taynton, for I know that in the end Jonas would discover some way to compel me. His mind is set upon this marriage, and he brooks no obstacles in his path."

'No," Charity agreed grimly, "he does not, so consider what would befall Mordisford if you fled together and did not win free. Jonas would have his life!"

"He would not dare! He is too great a coward to cross swords with Hal."

"You think there is no other way? Jonas is rich and influential, and so is Mr Taynton, who to save himself from ridicule would have to support him. They would have Mordisford flung into prison, and hanged, as like as not, on a trumped-up charge of abduction."

"You are trying to frighten me," Sarah said resentfully, "but it will not serve. If what you say is true, then 'tis even more urgent to escape without delay, before Jonas hears of Hal's arrival."

"Do you suppose he does not know of it already? If William saw Mordisford ride through the village, others must have done likewise, and from Dr Malperne to Jonas is a short step indeed."

"I am leaving this house tonight," Sarah replied stubbornly. "I am going, and you cannot stop me."

"Can I not?" Charity set the baby down again and turned to face her. "One whisper of this to Jonas or to my aunt, and you will speedily find yourself behind locked doors."

"You would not do that!" Sarah's voice was incredulous. "You are not capable of such treachery!"

"I do not wish to do it," Charity admitted, "but I would account it no treachery to keep you from a folly which could well shatter more lives than your own. I have already pointed out to you the danger to Mordisford which lies in this mad scheme, and if you truly love him, that should be enough. If it is not, and you think my threat to warn Jonas an idle one, consider this! Your brother has watched and waited for years for an opportunity to destroy Darrell, and if you go to the Dower House tonight you may be placing that opportunity within his reach."

"That is absurd! It is to Hal I shall be going, not to Sir Darrell."

"It is to Darrell's house, and Jonas will find some way to involve him, of that you may be sure." Charity came close to her cousin and gripped her by the shoulders, looking down into her face. "Understand this, Sarah! There is no one who comes before Darrell in my heart, nothing I would not do to shield him from harm! Do not force me to prove that to you!"

For a few seconds Sarah continued to stare at her, frightened in spite of herself by the intensity of Charity's low voice, the look in her dark eyes. Suddenly this cousin with whom she had grown up and to whom she was bound by such strong ties of affection and understanding seemed like a stranger. She jerked herself free and dropped on to a stool, covering her face with her hands.

"Then what am I to do? How can I even learn what

Hal intends, if you will not allow me to go to him?"

Charity hesitated for a moment, looking with troubled eyes at the huddled, despairing figure. Her resolve to keep Sarah at the Moat House was unshakable, yet it was clear that matters could not be left as they were. What Hal would decide to do she could not guess, but she felt certain that if he were prevented from communicating with Sarah, not even Darrell would be able to restrain him from some act of folly.

"If you will give me your solemn promise to make no attempt to leave," she said at length, "I will go to the Dower House myself and speak with him. Will that content you?"

Sarah raised her head and for a long moment they regarded each other in silence. Then Sarah said reluctantly:

"I will do so, Charity, if you make me a promise in return. Give me your word that you will not try to dissuade him from coming to my aid."

There was another pause, and then Charity said with a sigh: "Very well, child, you have my promise. The decision shall be his alone."

## II

The promise wrested from Sarah proved to be unnecessary, for Charity had guessed correctly that Hal's arrival could not remain unknown to Jonas. Quite soon after the conversation in the nursery he summoned Sarah to him, curtly informed her of it, and warned her that any attempt to leave the house would result in her instant imprisonment. Charity, hearing of this, half expected some curb upon her own freedom, but none was imposed, and later that evening she was able to make her escape undetected and unhindered.

When she reached the Dower House, Darrell's body-servant, John Parrish, admitted her. Stepping into the hall, she said softly:

"Is Mr Mordisford here, Parrish?"

"He arrived this afternoon, madam, and is with Sir Darrell now," the man replied. He seemed about to add more, but Charity had seen a gleam of light from beneath a closed door on the other side of the hall, and with a brief word of thanks went quickly forward and into the room.

Darrell was leaning against the side of the fireplace, the light from the candles above and behind him bright on his hair, and Hal Mordisford lounged in a chair on the other side of the hearth. Between them, another, older man sat facing the fire. He was dressed like a servant, but it was clear from his presence there, and from the respect with which his companions were listening to him, that this could be no more than a disguise.

Charity stopped short, staring in dismay as they all turned towards her, and then Darrell came quickly forward, taking her hands to kiss them, and smiling into her eyes. She said in a whisper:

"I did not know! We heard only that Mr Mordisford was here."

"It is no matter, sweetheart! Come!" He turned and led her towards the others, who had risen to greet her. "We are honoured by the presence of Colonel Nayland, who comes to me bearing His Majesty's commission and commands. Colonel, I am happy to have an opportunity to make Miss Shenfield known to you."

Colonel Nayland bowed. There was a courtliness in his manner which belied his humble attire.

"The honour, madam, is entirely mine. It is not often that our counsels are graced by a lady's presence."

She met his gaze frankly. "Had I known, sir, that such counsels were in progress I would not have ventured to intrude. If you wish it, I will withdraw."

He shook his head. "I am informed, Miss Shenfield, that you are in Sir Darrell's confidence, and your right to be here is unquestionable. It is my duty, however, to warn you of the perils which beset the path you have chosen to tread."

She faced him with the utmost composure, a faint challenge in her eyes. "To tread a perilous path in good company, sir, is surely better than to bide safely at home with the faint-hearted. May not a woman be as eager as a man to serve the King?"

The answer seemed to please him, and when she had greeted Hal, the Colonel himself placed a chair for her, and explained briefly that he and Mordisford had just come from Jersey, where a Royalist garrison was still holding out and where the King himself had arrived in mid-September.

"It is fortunate that Mr Mordisford has a kinsman and friends in the West Country," he added, "for it is here that my business lies, and in the guise of his servant I am less likely to be recognised than if I travelled alone. His Majesty has great hopes of support from the West, where the tradition of loyalty burns so brightly, and what I have learned from Sir Darrell seems to me an earnest that those hopes are justified."

"None the less," Darrell said soberly, "the fact remains that no matter how successful our plotting, the

English Cavaliers alone cannot hope to prevail against the Army. His Majesty will need to bring strong support from overseas."

"That much at least is already agreed upon. Aid is being sought in many quarters, from the King of France, from William of Orange, in Germany and in Denmark. There is also a powerful faction, led by Her Majesty the Queen Mother, which favours a Scots alliance."

"Scotland?" The exclamation was wrenched from Charity's lips. "The Scots supported Parliament against the late King, and surrendered him to his enemies when he placed himself under their protection. Moreover, they suffered a crushing defeat last year at Cromwell's hands."

"All this is true, madam, and yet scarcely a week after the late King's death his son was proclaimed in Scotland, and many believe that from Scotland will come the means to restore him to the English throne. That such an alliance would be unpopular among His Majesty's loyal supporters here is a fact well recognised, but, as Sir Darrell has truly said, those supporters cannot hope to prevail alone."

Charity was silent, perceiving the justice of his words and yet unable to conquer a feeling of dismay. She looked at Darrell, and saw in his eyes a reflection of her own repugnance. The misgivings which she had felt ever since Hal's visit in the spring, and which she had loyally endeavoured to stifle, roused themselves again, more vigorously than before.

Colonel Nayland was speaking again. "These are matters which do not rest in our hands. Our task is to help to create an organisation which, when the time comes, will be ready and able to lead a general rising in support of His Majesty, and such a task is no simple matter. Secrecy is of the utmost importance yet far from easy to maintain. Our enemies are fully alive to the dangers of Royalist conspiracy, they are well served by spies and informers, and their control of the mails makes it possible for them to intercept letters and decipher them." He paused, looking from one to the other of the two younger men. "Suspicion is fatally easy to arouse, and in these times suspicion alone can mean arrest, imprisonment and the wreckage of such designs as we are engaged upon."

Hal made an impatient movement. "Sir, these things we knew and accepted when we resolved to continue active in the service of the King."

"True, Mr Mordisford, but a wise man constantly reminds himself of them. Danger of discovery can lurk anywhere, sometimes in places where we least expect it."

"For every person in this house I would vouch with my life," Darrell said slowly, "and for most of those in the village also; but there are some . . ." he paused, looking at Charity as though wondering how much to disclose.

"There are some who would like nothing better than to strike at those who serve the King," she concluded calmly. "My kinsman, Jonas Shenfield; his servant and familiar, Daniel Stotewood; the preacher, Dr Malperne. Very little happens in Conyngton St John that one or other of those three does not discover." She glanced at Hal. "Jonas is already aware, for example, of your arrival."

He shrugged. "That does not matter. It is safe that

I should come openly, since I have good reason for my visit."

She glanced at Darrell, an unspoken question in her eyes, and he shook his head.

"I have told him nothing."

Charity hesitated for a moment, aware of Hal's sudden stillness, the frowning question of his glance, and then she turned to Colonel Nayland. "Sir, you will have realised by now that if I visit this house I have to come secretly and in haste. Since time presses, will you forgive me if I speak now of a family matter?"

"Madam, it would be discourteous in me to do aught else. If the matter is private, I will leave you."

She shook her head, frowning a little. "I think, sir, that you would do well to stay. What I have to tell Mr Mordisford may concern you more closely than you suppose."

"In the fiend's name, Miss Charity, what is there to tell?" Hal broke in impatiently. "Has any harm befallen Sarah? Is she ill?"

"She is in excellent health," Charity replied, and hesitated, looking at him with troubled eyes. "My friend, a cruel blow is best dealt swiftly. Sarah is to be married two days hence."

He went white, and a look came into his eyes from which she was obliged to avert her own. After an interminable pause he said with difficulty: "Married to whom?"

"To Edward Taynton, a gentleman of Plymouth." Charity kept her gaze fixed upon the blazing fire, her voice carefully empty of all expression. "He is older than she, a widower, rich and influential. It is an excellent match."

"An excellent match!" There was a world of contempt in Hal's bitter voice. "Excellent for whom? For her bullying renegade of a brother? Never tell me that Sarah herself is willing!"

"No, she has resisted the marriage with every means in her power, and now, learning of your arrival, believes that you have come to save her."

"And so I shall!" He sprang to his feet, his face still pale, but set now in lines of determination. "I will have her away from them, cost what it may!"

"It may cost your life," Darrell warned him. "We know that Shenfield is an arrant coward, but Taynton, so I have heard, is a brave man and skilled in the use of arms."

"Am I to hang back therefore, yielding Sarah to him without striking a blow in her defence? That is not the counsel, Darrell, I would expect from you!"

"Mr Mordisford!" Colonel Nayland's quiet voice broke in sternly upon the impassioned words. "I have heard enough, I think, to tell why Miss Shenfield bade me stay. Have you so soon forgotten the mission which brought us back to England?"

That Hal had forgotten it was made evident by the utter dismay which flooded into his face at the rebuke. He stared blankly at Nayland, and the Colonel looked grimly back.

"We came here to work for the Cause, work to which we pledged ourselves in the presence of the King himself. No private concern, however urgent, must be permitted to endanger our errand. To allow it to do so would be tantamount to treason."

Hal sank slowly back into the chair from which he had just risen. His face was ashen now, and sweat beaded his brow. "She looks to me to save her!" he said desperately. "I cannot betray her trust!"

"Would you betray instead the trust which His Majesty has reposed in you?" Nayland demanded ruthlessly. "Your life is no longer your own to gamble with —you have pledged it to the service of the King." He paused, regarding Hal with an expression not entirely lacking in sympathy. "My friend, you have not given the matter due consideration, for, believe me, there is no place for a wife in the kind of life to which you and I are committed."

"But what in God's name am I to do? What am I to tell her?"

"You can tell her nothing! As I reminded you not long since, secrecy is of the utmost importance, and to confide in the young lady would imperil all of us. The only safe course, as I see it, is to remove hence without delay, for if her brother knows of your presence he will be on his guard, and may well move against you without knowing the real worth of the quarry he hunts." He turned to Darrell. "Did you not speak, sir, of a loyal gentleman living near Exeter?"

"Yes, Sir Richard Linslade of Dorringford. He and Mordisford are known to each other, and he will gladly give you shelter."

Hal gave a groan and buried his face in his hands, thrusting his fingers deep into his long hair. "Merciful God, what a choice to be thrust upon a man! A choice between betrayal and betrayal!"

Colonel Nayland got up and laid a hand upon the bowed shoulder. His voice was unexpectedly compassionate. "My young friend, there *is* no choice! Your first loyalty and duty is to His Majesty, no matter what dear hopes or proud ambitions must be sacrificed therefore."

## III

The next day was one such as only October could show. The sun shone with the brilliance if not the warmth of high summer, and beneath a sky of vivid, wind-scoured blue lay a countryside painted with all the glowing colours of autumn. It was a joyous day, as though the guttering candle of the year burned brightest of all just before extinction, but Charity, watching Sarah's face as the coach bore them down the hill on their way to church, thought that to her the brightness must seem a cruel mockery.

Her own mind still shrank from the memory of the previous night, when she had come back from the Dower House to break the news to Sarah that Hal's return could change nothing, that he was as powerless to help her as she was to help herself. It had not been easy to tell, just as it had not been easy for Hal himself to write the letter she carried with her, and her heart ached with pity for them both. She had tried to soften the blow, to warn Sarah of what the letter contained, but the girl would pay no heed, and snatched it from her to tear it open with trembling hands.

Charity watched her read it, saw the eagerness in her face turn to dismay, to horror and finally to outright disbelief. Sarah crushed the paper between her hands and turned a white, accusing face towards her cousin.

"This is your doing! You did not keep your word!"

Charity shook her head. "Neither my doing, Sarah,

nor Darrell's, that I swear to you."

"But it cannot be true! Hal would not desert me so!" Sarah's voice quivered piteously on the verge of tears. She held the letter out in a trembling hand. "He uses here the very arguments with which you sought to dissuade me. Would he do that unless you had also laid them before him?"

"The truth is the truth, child," Charity replied gently. "It has been there all the while for one not wilfully blind to read."

It had taken a long time to convince Sarah, and longer still to comfort the passion of despair which conviction brought with it, and it had been very late when at last she sank into exhausted sleep. This morning she was pale and quiet, with dark shadows beneath her eyes, yet Charity had an uneasy feeling that in spite of everything she had not completely abandoned hope. Perhaps she would not do so until she was actually Edward Taynton's wife.

In the church they were all aware of the speculative glances of the villagers, of a curiosity which quivered in the air like a tangible thing. Only Sarah seemed indifferent to it. From the moment they entered the church she remained with bowed head and downcast eyes, praying perhaps, Charity thought compassionately, for the miracle in which now lay her sole hope. Only when Darrell's firm footstep sounded on the stone floor did she stir, swinging round with sudden eagerness in her face, an eagerness which faded as swiftly as it had come when she saw that he was alone.

Throughout the prayers and the lengthy sermon, even while the banns of marriage were read for the third and final time, she remained as impassive as a statue.

Charity was uneasy, waiting for she knew not what, and was thankful when at last they came out of the quiet, cold church into the sunshine. They walked along the path to the lych-gate; Jonas and Ellen, Mrs Shenfield and Sarah, Charity herself in her usual humble place at the rear, and Jonas handed first his wife and then his mother into the coach.

It needed considerable effort and some assistance from Jonas and a stalwart manservant to hoist Mrs Shenfield's bulk into the coach. Charity, waiting beside Sarah, watched Darrell come along the path towards them and thought, with pity and with gratitude, that in spite of all they were still more fortunate than Hal and Sarah. Their glances met for a moment, and then as he turned towards the place where his horses was tethered, Sarah stepped forward and spoke his name.

Astonishment halted him in his tracks. Jonas swung round towards them, and servants and villagers turned to stare. Sarah paid no heed to any of them.

"Sir Darrell," she said again, quiet desperation throbbing in her voice. "Where is Mr Mordisford?"

He looked at her, and she saw compassion in the hazel eyes. "He has gone, Miss Sarah," he said quietly. "He came but to bid me farewell, for he has obtained leave to travel beyond the seas, and intends to dwell henceforth in France."

Those who watched her saw Sarah's last hope die. She stood very still, with white face and stricken eyes, while the jovial October wind shook the trees, and golden leaves fluttered about her and swirled around her feet. Then Darrell bowed and turned away, and Charity stepped forward and laid her hand gently on

Sarah's arm. Obedient to the touch, moving like a sleepwalker, she allowed herself to be guided to the coach and helped up into its dark interior.

During the journey back to the Moat House she sat like one stunned, indifferent both to her mother's scolding and the silent sympathy of Charity and Ellen. Even when the house was reached she showed no reaction, but followed them into the hall and walked across to the fireplace, where she stood staring down at the blazing logs.

"So, Sarah!" Jonas's voice at length broke harshly into the long silence. "You see now how purposeless your defiance has been! The brave gallant to whom you vowed eternal constancy deserts you, and departs in haste lest to linger place him in danger of punishment. Are your eyes open at last to his true worth? Are you ready now to obey me?"

His sister did not immediately reply. She put a hand to the bosom of her gown and drew out a folded paper which Charity recognised as Hal's letter. Without looking at it Sarah crumpled it in her hands and dropped it on to the fire. As the flames began to lick around it she turned at last to face her brother.

"I am ready, Jonas," she said listlessly. "There is nothing left now for which to strive."

# 7

CHARITY stood by the broken fountain at Conyngton and felt a fleeting delight in the scented sweetness of the July morning. During seven years of neglect the gardens had run riot into a tangled wilderness, but flowers still bloomed there and close to where she stood the shaggy, untrimmed yew hedge was smothered with roses red as blood, their petals still wet with dew where the early sunlight had not reached them.

She leaned her hands on the rim of the discoloured marble basin and stared at her reflection in the pool of rain-water it held. This was her twenty-third birthday, and by the standards of her day she could be considered well past her first youth. The image in the pool stared uncompromisingly back at her, the dark, aquiline face appearing older and more severe than need be because of the austere white cap which framed it so closely. With sudden, resentful impatience she pulled off the cap and unpinned her hair so that it tumbled down, thick, straight and heavy, to fall below her waist like a glossy, blue-black cloak. She gathered a cluster of the roses, fastened them at her breast and turned again to the pool. This time a gipsy looked back at her, sullen and defiant, so that a wry smile curved her lips even though tears stung her eyes.

Behind her mirrored face another reflection took shape, and she spun round with a gasp to find herself in Darrell's arms. He held her lightly, looking down at her, and she knew with a swift surge of reassurance that in his eyes, at least, she was beautiful.

" 'Tis years since I saw you with your hair about your shoulders," he said softly. "You look now as you did when you were a child."

"Would that I were!" she murmured. "Oh, if we could turn back time, and be children again!"

He pulled her closer and kissed her, long and ardently, and then looked at her again as she lay back against his shoulder, her lips parted, the dark eyes languorous beneath heavy lids.

"Would you, Charity?" he challenged her gently. "Would you indeed wish to go back?"

She sighed. "No, my love, that was folly! But to escape from the present, from the cold, harsh ugliness which is thrust upon me—ah, Darrell, how I hunger sometimes for laughter, for beauty, for the colour and richness of life! For this," she touched the roses she wore, and then the dark, coarse stuff of her gown, "rather than this."

"And you shall have it, my heart! Before God, I swear it!" He saw her eyes mist again with tears, and added urgently: "Do not lose faith now, little one, when you have endured so bravely for so long. We shall find a way!"

She nodded, smiling through her tears, trying to banish the doubts and the despair that plagued her, or at least to hide them from him. "Forgive me, Darrell!

I know not what ails me this day, save that it is so long since I saw you, and I fear for your safety whenever you are away. You know that already Jonas suspects you."

"Suspect what he may, I provided myself with a sound reason to account for this last visit to Exeter, and though I met with Linslade and some others there, no man alive could prove that it was anything more than a mere friendly gathering. Have I not given you my word to take no undue risk? Come, let us sit down and I will tell you what news I bring, but first I have a gift for you."

He led her to a stone bench which stood, half hidden in rank grass, a few yards away, and when they were seated took a ring from his little finger. It appeared to be one delicately wrought band, but when she looked more closely she saw that it was a gimmal ring, consisting of two separate hoops cunningly joined together. Darrell parted them, and took her hand to place one hoop on her finger, returning the other to his own.

"On the day we are wed," he said gently, "the two shall be joined again to make your marriage-ring. Until then, wear one for me, as I shall wear the other for you, to serve as a pledge and a proof of our love."

"I need no ring as proof of that, Darrell, but I shall treasure your gift as my dearest possession."

"It is of no great value," he said ruefully. "I would rather you had the ruby which was my mother's, but since you so steadfastly refuse it, I found this for you instead."

"Your mother's jewels, and Alison's, belong to Conyngton, my dear. We decided on that long ago."

"*You* decided on it, little one," he replied with a

trace of humour, "but we will argue no more of it. God knows I would have been hard put to it these three years past to contrive without them!"

"You said that you bring news from Exeter," she said after a pause. "What has been passing in the world while I have been mewed up at the Moat House, tending Ellen and the new babe?"

"Much of great moment, though whether for good or ill, no man can tell." His voice was grave, and he frowned a little as he spoke. "A month ago, the King landed in Scotland. He had been in Breda since March, arguing terms with the Scottish commissioners, but the treaty was not finally signed until May."

She cast him a shrewd glance. "This alliance with the Scots disturbs you, does it not?"

He nodded. "As it must disturb all who hold the same belief as I. To make terms with the Covenanters is to betray the cause to which His Majesty's father was faithful unto death; to look for support to the English Presbyterians is to antagonize those in this kingdom who have hitherto been most ready to risk all for the King. Though this treaty may be prompted by counsels of despair, by the failure to find help in any other quarter, 'tis hard to see how any lasting good can come of it."

"But if the King can regain his throne, even with the help of the Scots, then, surely, the end will justify the means?"

"*If* he can do so!" Darrell replied dubiously. "No dependence can be placed upon the ability of the Scots to defeat the Ironside army."

Silence fell upon them. Charity sat, her hand in Darrell's, and stared at the blackened, crumbling walls of Conyngton looming bleakly above the heavy foliage of high summer. The shadow of them lay across the fountain and the tumbling roses, and, so it seemed, across her heart also. She knew that in the past months, Royalist plotting in the West had prospered. There was now a chain of conspiracy, called the Western Association and led by Lord Beauchamp, the son of the Marquis of Hertford, which stretched from Cornwall to Hampshire and northwards into Gloucester and Herefordshire. Yet even while this web of conspiracy was being precariously woven, there had been signs that the Commonwealth authorities were on their guard. The Council of State was well served by spies and informers, and now, with war threatening in Scotland, was unlikely to relax its vigilance in the notoriously Royalist West.

"I met with Hal in Exeter!" Darrell's voice broke abruptly into her troubled thoughts. "He came with letters from my lord Beauchamp, and to gather such information as we could give him."

"So he is in England again!" Charity said thoughtfully. "Or did he never leave, in spite of what you told Sarah that day?"

"He left, though not as soon as I let her believe. He went back to Jersey, and has since been in Holland also. His whole life, it seems, is now dedicated to the service of the King."

"Did he seek news of Sarah?"

"No, nor could I have given him any, save that she has been married to Edward Taynton these nine months. I know no more than that."

"Nor I!" Charity's voice was troubled. "I have had no word from her since Mr Taynton took her to Plymouth. I fear sometimes that she holds me to blame for what befell, yet Ellen, against whom she can bear no grudge at all, has fared the same. Though only a few miles separate us, we might well be upon opposite sides of the world."

"Yet her mother must have news of her, and Jonas is often in Plymouth."

"They tell us nothing, either of Sarah or any other matter. We could be prisoners in the Moat House for all we know of happenings outside its walls," Charity said with a sigh. "No doubt it is but another instance of Jonas's petty spite, which now seems to be turned as often against his wife as against me."

"Even now, when she has just borne him another son?"

Charity nodded. "Even now! Jonas has no affection for her, nor for his children. Hatred rules his life, and seems to have consumed by its intensity all gentler emotions." She sighed again, withdrew her hand from his, and began to bind up her hair. "Dearest, I must go now! It was hard enough to steal even these few brief moments from the tasks I have to do."

He started to protest, realised the futility of it and lapsed into silence, watching sombrely while she coiled up the heavy hair and covered it again with the nun-like coif. Then she unfastened the roses and stood for a second or two with them in her hands, looking down at them.

"How I wish I might wear these still, and so carry one small part of the beauty of the summer with me, but Jonas and my aunt would condemn me for vanity."

She laid the flowers in the shallow water in the fountain, touching the glowing petals gently with one finger. Darrell, who had risen and come to her side, said in a bantering tone which did not quite succeed in masking his deep feeling:

"When we are wed, you shall have a satin gown the colour of those roses, and not a Puritan in all England shall say you nay!"

"That is a rash promise, sir, and I shall hold you to it," she was beginning lightly, but his sudden frown, the hard, warning grip of his hand on hers, smote her into silence. Somewhere close by, a stick snapped beneath an unwary foot.

## II

Darrell drew his sword and stepped forward so that he stood between Charity and the place whence the sound had come. He said sharply: "Who is there?"

There was a pause, which lasted no longer than a heartbeat and yet which seemed to Charity to drag on for ever, and then the undergrowth parted and a man emerged. A short, plump man, inconspicuously dressed, with a round, pink face like an elderly and cunning cherub.

"Put up your sword, Sir Darrell," he said placatingly. "You know that you have naught to fear from me."

"Japhet Chawton!" Anger and astonishment mingled in Darrell's voice, but he sheathed the sword again as he had been bidden. "What in the fiend's name do you here?"

"I sought you, sir!" The man's glance slid past him to Charity, standing silent and watchful in the background. He bowed. "Your pardon, madam, for this intrusion, but I have business with Sir Darrell."

"Is it business so urgent that it could not await my return to the Dower House?"

Mr Chawton made an apologetic gesture. "It is not desperate, Sir Darrell, but better for all of us if I do not linger too long in this neighbourhood. Mr Shenfield, I understand, is quick to learn of the presence of strangers in the village."

"True, Mr Chawton, and you would therefore have been wiser to stay close within the Dower House. There you would have been seen by none save my servants, who are completely trustworthy." The words were pleasant enough, but there was an underlying note of annoyance in Darrell's voice. "Be good enough to return there now, and I will join you directly."

Japhet Chawton bowed again to Charity, and then turned and vanished into the tangled undergrowth. When the sound of his going had faded, Charity said in a low voice:

"Darrell, who is that man?"

He shrugged slightly. "One who serves the Cause by carrying messages and performing similar errands. I do not greatly like him, but in such enterprises as we are engaged upon, one must use the tools which come most readily to hand."

She frowned. "Are you certain that he is to be trusted? He is not a Devon man."

"No, he comes from Somerset, but that is no good reason for distrusting him. He came well furnished with credentials from the Royalist leaders in that county, and has since proved his usefulness in many ways. Be easy, sweetheart! I trust no man farther than I must."

With that she knew that she must be content, and said no more as they walked slowly towards the gatehouse. As they passed within sight of the remains of the manor they saw that a fresh gap had been torn in the decaying walls, and that a great pile of masonry now blocked the terrace and spilled into the garden below. That it was newly fallen was evident from the branches it had dragged down with it and which protruded in many places from the tumbled stone, their leaves withering but not yet dead.

"It must have fallen during the storm two nights since," Darrell said with a sigh. "The walls grow more dangerous day by day. Never venture within them, my love, for they could prove to be the veriest death-trap."

"Be sure that I will not," she replied with a shiver. "There is naught there now to lure me." She broke off, a puzzled frown creasing her brow. "Darrell, how did Mr Chawton know that he would find you here?"

Darrell frowned also. "Yes, that is strange! It may be that he did not know, and that mere curiosity brought him here, but I shall inquire into the matter none the less. I have no liking for being spied upon, even by my own associates."

Charity sighed and did not pursue the subject, although to remain silent did some violence to her feelings. She knew that in active sedition Darrell had found a release from frustration and from the sense of uselessness which had oppressed him, but though her own instinct was to fight rather than surrender, and meekness and patience were forced upon her nature rather than inherent in it, she could not conquer the anxieties born of her great love for him. Yet she had promised at the outset not to seek to turn him from his purpose, and, cost her what it might, she meant to keep her word.

At the gatehouse they parted and Charity walked quickly across the park and down the path through the woods, wondering as she went what errand had brought Japhet Chawton to Conyngton that day. She knew very little of the actual details of the conspiracy, or what part Darrell and his companions played in the larger design which now encompassed the whole West Country. Perhaps, she thought wryly, it would be better to know nothing at all; to live, as her cousin Beth Linslade lived, in happy ignorance of the perilous enterprise upon which the men were engaged. Yet had she not known, it was unlikely that she would have discovered that Jonas's ready suspicions had been aroused.

Her thoughts went back to the day, six months ago, when a January gale had been driving icy rains across the grey, winter countryside, and Ellen, coming to the nursery, had remarked idly that Dr Malperne chose inclement weather to come visiting. The preacher, she added in answer to Charity's question, had just arrived to see Jonas. She seemed to think that the matter warranted no further comment, but Charity could not share this placid acceptance of Malperne's arrival. He was a fairly frequent visitor at the Moat House, but something unusual must surely have happened to bring him all the way from the village on such a day. She made an excuse to leave the nursery, and hurried along the passages and down the stairs.

The big, stone-flagged hall was empty, lit only by the dim greyness filtering in through the high windows, and the flickering light of the logs burning on the hearth, but a gleam of candlelight showed beneath the closed door of the parlour. Charity crept close to the door and strained her ears, and after a few moments caught a few words in Jonas's familiar tones.

". . . known it before we might have learned something to the purpose. What use coming to me now, when all the birds have flown?"

"Yet I warrant, sir, that they will return!" That was the preacher's voice, harsh and carrying. "It cannot have been mere chance which brought them together here, since you tell me that similar meetings have already caused alarm in Plymouth."

"Aye, the malignants infest this county like a plague!" Jonas replied. "And you may depend upon it that Conyngton is in the forefront of their damnable conspiracies."

"And where he leads, the rest of this parish will follow," Malperne added bitterly. "These people pay no heed to warnings and admonitions, but ape stupidity, and feign to know nothing of what is done at the Dower House."

"Let *me* but discover what is done there, and you shall see them dance to a different tune!" The vindictiveness in Jonas's voice was unmistakable. "If treason is being plotted there it is our clear duty to discover it, and, with the Lord's guidance, discover it we shall."

The sound of a footfall on the stairs, and the glimmer of an approaching candle, had at that point forced Charity to abandon her place of vantage, but she had heard enough to send her hurrying to the Dower House at the first opportunity, for this was a warning she dare not entrust to Polly. There she learned that the incident which had aroused Malperne's suspicions was a meeting which had taken place there a few days before under the disguise of a hunting-party. When she heard this, Charity stared at Darrell in dismay.

"Is it wise to meet here, with Jonas and his spies so close at hand?"

He sighed. "It seemed safe enough, but if Jonas is suspicious, some other meeting-place must be found. I should be failing in my duty if I knowingly allowed the Cause to be endangered."

Charity was more concerned that he should not endanger himself, but knew that any hint of this would not be well received. She tried to comfort herself with the knowledge that the conspirators would foregather no more at the Dower House, and that as long as they met elsewhere Jonas was less likely to discover them, but still she could not be wholly reassured. Such discovery would mean for Darrell imprisonment and ruin, or even a traitor's death. That nightmare knowledge was with her always, a hideous, threatening shadow which dominated her whole life.

### III

Charity had not exaggerated when she told Darrell that she and Ellen were little better than prisoners at the Moat House. Their world was bounded by the garden and the park, their lives by the busy round of domestic tasks. Only when the whole household attended church on the Sabbath did they go as far as the village, and then there was no chance to linger, or to speak with anyone other than Dr Malperne.

Thrust so much into each other's company—for Charity now found herself acting as waiting-gentlewoman to Ellen as well as being in charge of the nursery—the two young women had become good friends, and Charity was as happy as she could ever hope to be in her kinsman's house. Some months earlier she had found it necessary to explain to Ellen the circumstances of her long-standing betrothal to Darrell, but though the younger woman had been sympathetic Charity felt quite certain that she was incapable of real understanding. Ellen, terrified of her husband, unable even to feel respect for him, could not even imagine a love of the kind which bound Charity and Darrell to each other.

When Charity entered the nursery that summer morning, she found Ellen there, the new baby at her breast. He was now six weeks old, a bonny boy for whom Jonas had chosen the name of Oliver, but though the babe was thriving, it seemed to Charity that the mother was not. Ellen's face was pale and drawn, and there were dark shadows beneath her eyes.

One reason for this depression was not far to seek. Soon after Oliver's birth one of Ellen's married brothers had come from Plymouth bearing gifts and good wishes from the Pennan family, but when Ellen asked eagerly for news of Tom, he had been evasive, and promised only that she would be told as soon as such news reached them. From talk heard later at table, Charity gathered that Captain Pennan's ship had been expected home in the early spring, and that its failure to appear was causing some anxiety. Charity herself heard this with dismay. The perils of seafaring were many, and it was not pleasant to think that Tom Pennan might have fallen victim to one of them.

Yet even anxiety on behalf of a dearly loved brother was scarcely enough to account for all Ellen's unhappiness. Something else was weighing heavily upon her mind, and for some time Charity had been waiting for a suitable occasion to ask her what was wrong. Later that day an ideal opportunity at last presented itself. They were at work together in the still-room, reasonably safe from any danger of interruption, and Charity, after silently studying her companion's downcast face for several moments, said abruptly:

"Ellen, what ails you? You have been grievously troubled for a long while now." Ellen did not reply, and after a moment's pause Charity went on persuasively: "Child, you know that you may safely confide in me, and that if it is in my power to help you, I will."

"No one can help me!" Ellen's voice was flat, with a complete lack of expression which was shocking, and she did not look at Charity as she spoke. "Yet perhaps simply to talk of it may make the things easier to bear. Cousin, there are times when my husband is tormented by evil dreams, when he cries out in terror, thinking he is in hell and suffering the tortures of eternal damnation. When first we were married I tried to talk to him about it, being foolish enough to think that I might bring him comfort, but this merely provoked a terrible anger in him, and he forbade me ever to speak of it again. Nor have I done so, to him or to anyone else, until now."

Charity regarded her with a frown. "That Jonas's conscience may be thus burdened I can believe, but it is no fault of yours. You have brooded too much over it."

"There is something more!" Ellen's face was still averted, her hands moving nervously among the various vessels on the table before her. "Something of which Jonas himself is not aware! At such times I have heard him cry out a name, a woman's name." Without warning, her gaze came swiftly to meet Charity's. "Alison! Was not Sir Darrell Conyngton's wife so called?"

Charity stood very still, staring at her in blank dismay. She knew that Darrell himself was convinced that Jonas had cherished a secret passion for Alison, and now it seemed that he was right. For Ellen's sake Charity wished she could deny it, but could tell from the other girl's expression that she had already betrayed herself.

"That was her name," she said carefully, "but she had been at Conyngton for less than a year when Jonas went to live in Plymouth, and in that time I doubt whether they met more than half a dozen times. Alison was devoted to Darrell and completely happy in her marriage."

"Yet Jonas desired her," Ellen said stubbornly, and made an impatient gesture as Charity started to speak. "Spare your protests, cousin, for this is something I know beyond all doubt. A ghost stands between my husband and me, and when he looks at me or touches me, I know that he despises me because I am not Alison." She leaned forward, adding with sudden urgency: "Charity, what was she like? I have to know!"

What was she like? Charity's mind flew back across the years for an instant the memory of Alison was as vivid as though she stood before them. Alison, timid and gentle as a fawn, and as beautiful, with her fragile bones and silvery-gold hair and dark grey eyes. Then the memory faded and she was looking again at Ellen, who was also small and fair, but had no claim at all to beauty.

"Why?" she asked bluntly. "So that the ghost may

have a face and a form as well as a name? No, Ellen, I will not tell you! If what you suppose is true—and it may be, although we have no means of knowing—Jonas did no more than admire Alison from afar, and she was dead five years before he married you. Why torment yourself by dwelling morbidly upon the thought of her?"

"There is another thought which I cannot put from my mind," Ellen replied in a low voice. "A dreadful question to which I can find no answer. Jonas has always hated Sir Darrell, and I am certain that he desired Sir Darrell's wife. Lady Conyngton was alone and unprotected when Jonas led the soldiers to plunder the manor. Charity, the thought which fills me with horror is—what did he intend towards her? What outrage might he not have committed had you not had the wit to seek safety here?"

There was a considerable pause before Charity replied. The same question had crossed her own mind many times, but she knew that it could never be answered, and it was profitless to dwell upon what might have happened when the reality was tragic and terrible enough. She moved closer to Ellen and laid a comforting arm about her shoulders.

"My dear, this is to no purpose at all! I know, none better, how heavy a cross you have to bear, and I wish with all my heart that I could lighten it for you, but there is so little that I or anyone else can do. I can only counsel you to keep a brave heart for the sake of the little ones, and to strive, hard though it be, to feel compassion for their father. Above all, do not plague yourself with fruitless speculation about what is past. Whatever crime was contemplated that day must lie, like that which was committed, between Jonas and his conscience. That, at least, is a burden you have no need to share."

# 8

A WEEK later Charity was passing that part of the garden which offered a glimpse of the track leading across the park to the road when she caught sight of a solitary horseman approaching. Curiosity prompted her to pause, but as he drew nearer this was overwhelmed by a keener interest, and she walked quickly to meet him. A few moments were sufficient to make suspicion a certainty. It was Tom Pennan who came riding towards her.

He drew rein beside her and sprang from the saddle, sweeping off his hat to bow before taking the hand she put out to him in greeting. She said with a smile:

"This is a glad surprise, Captain Pennan, and one we have long hoped for. I am heartily pleased to see you safely home."

"And I heartily pleased to be here, Miss Charity! I reached Plymouth but two days since and came here with as little delay as possible, for my brother told me that Ellen was fretting for news of me."

"She did indeed fear greatly that some mischance had befallen you." Charity, looking at him as he stood bareheaded before her, perceived that he was thinner than before, his tanned face hollow-cheeked, a fresh scar slanting across his brow and vanishing beneath the sun-bleached hair which now showed here and there a thread of silver. After a moment she added quietly, "And I think, sir, that those fears were not altogether unfounded."

He laughed, falling into step beside her as they went towards the house. "Not altogether," he agreed. "We were upon our homeward course when we fell foul of a Spanish ship of twice our armament, and had a hard fight of it before we could win free. Five of my men were killed and another half-score wounded, myself among them, while the ship had taken such hurt that we had to go limping into the nearest friendly port to lick our wounds."

" 'No peace beyond the line,' " Charity said lightly, quoting words she had heard him use during his previous visit. "You have chosen a perilous calling, sir!"

"Perilous, but profitable," he retorted with a grin. "Spain takes more shrewd blows than she gives, and I would rather win gold at sword's point on the high seas than toil for it in the gloom of my father's counting-house."

She chuckled. "Mayhap, but I must remind you that it will be prudent not to say so to my kinsman."

By this time they had reached the house and there was no further opportunity for private conversation. Later, Ellen told Charity, with unconcealed delight, that it was Tom's intention to remain in England for some months. His health had suffered as a result of his recent wound and the fever which had followed it, and since he had already prospered considerably there was no reason why he should put to sea again before he had fully recovered. Charity wondered secretly how far the Captain's decision was a result of seeing his sister again. Joy at his return had brought colour to Ellen's cheeks and a sparkle to her eyes, but in spite of this the change in her must be marked and disturbing to one who had not seen her for over a year.

Two days later Charity was in the nursery when Tom walked into the room. She looked round quickly, a finger to her lips, for she had just succeeded in rocking the baby to sleep, and then, going across to him, she said softly:

"If you are seeking Ellen, sir, she is in the garden, and little Jonathan with her."

"I know!" He pitched his voice low, as she had done. "It is you, Miss Charity, with whom I wish to speak."

She was not surprised, guessing that he wanted to talk about Ellen, but she wondered with dismay how she could reassure him on that score. With another cautious glance towards the cradle she beckoned him across to the far side of the room, where a window set deep in the thick wall looked out upon the garden, and there turned to him with a look of silent inquiry.

To her surprise, he seemed to have some difficulty in choosing his words. He stood looking from the window, frowning and drumming his fingers on the wide sill, for so long that Charity began to grow impatient. At last, turning to her with an air of resolution, he said abruptly:

"You must know by now that I am a man to whom fine phrases do not come easily, and if what I have to say offends you, I can only ask your pardon." Again he hesitated, and this time she waited patiently, curious now to know what was to follow. "Miss Charity," he resumed at length, "I know that your situation in this house is an unhappy one. While I was away you were often in my thoughts, and at length I realised that it is in my power to offer you escape from a life which must be wellnigh intolerable. It is my hope, madam, that you will become my wife."

Charity gasped. Whatever she had expected it was certainly not this, and she could only stare at Tom in speechless stupefaction. Finding her silent, he plunged again into speech.

"I know, of course, that on this subject I should have approached Shenfield first, but in the circumstances, and since you and I are both of an age to know our own minds, it seemed simpler to come to a decision ourselves before consulting others. I will be frank with you, Miss Charity! The lot of a sailor's wife is not an easy one, for she must spend many weary months alone, not knowing with any certainty when, if ever, he will return; but you would be the mistress of your own household, and not a dependent in one where you are constantly slighted and misused. That, at least, I can give you—and my respect and admiration always."

Charity had by now recovered a little from her astonishment, and when Tom paused again she said gently: "You do me great honour, Captain Pennan! There are few men who would so generously offer marriage to a woman situated as I am, and I shall remember it always with the deepest gratitude, but it is not possible. You could not know it, but I have been promised these three years past." She saw astounded disbelief in his eyes, and added simply: "To Sir Darrell Conyngton."

There was no need for further explanation. After a long pause, Tom said in a low voice, "Does Shenfield know?"

"He knows, and you may imagine with what delight he has withheld his consent. His most cherished desire is to see Darrell dead and the estate of Conyngton in his own possession, but meanwhile he seizes eagerly upon any opportunity, great or small, to cause him hurt. That, sir, is the measure of his hatred!"

Tom was silent for a moment, compassionately studying her, his own disappointment overwhelmed by pity for her. "It is fortunate, then," he said at length, "that I did not speak of this to him. If he is indeed so eager to strike at Sir Darrell, he might have sought to compel you into an unwelcome marriage, as Ellen tells me he has compelled his sister. I could not have forgiven myself if I had thus unwittingly caused you further distress."

She shook her head, a faint, bitter smile touching her lips. "He would not do that, sir, while Darrell lives, for he fears that if I were forced to wed elsewhere, Darrell himself might take a second wife. It is Jonas's avowed intention to make himself squire, and master of all that once belonged to the Conyngtons, and that purpose would be harder to achieve if there were an heir."

"So while Shenfield lives you can have no hope of happiness, unless you go into exile and let him possess himself of the estate? Or unless by some miracle the King regains his own and Shenfield's authority can be broken. God defend us! Are you content to wait for that?"

"Content?" she repeated bitterly. "No, Captain Pennan, not content! We wait because we must, because there are those in Conyngton St John who would suffer from Jonas's malice if we fled." She sighed deeply, and leaned her head against the wall beside her. "We endure with such patience as we can command, but it is hard! Dear God in Heaven, how hard it is!"

"Shenfield is evil!" Tom said quietly. "He spreads sorrow and pain about him like a plague, and seems bent upon destroying those who should come foremost in his regard—Ellen, his sister, and yourself. I would there were some way I could help you, my dear."

She smiled a little, touched by his concern for her. "True friendship, sir, is always a source of strength and comfort," she said gently, "the more so to one whose friends are few. Believe me, I am very grateful!"

## II

Before Captain Pennan left the Moat House again, Charity had realised that there was a way in which he might help her, and so relieve her mind of at least one of the anxieties which pressed upon it. She confided to him her belief that Jonas was deliberately preventing any communication between her and Sarah, and asked him if he would visit Edward Taynton's house on her behalf.

"As you know, sir," she explained, "Sarah went unwillingly to her marriage, and though it is my earnest hope, and, indeed, my belief, that by now she may have found a measure of contentment, I would dearly like to be assured of it. There was much affection between us in the old days, and lacking any news at all, I cannot be easy about her."

"You shall have that news, Miss Charity," Tom promised her. "It will not be difficult to obtain, and you may depend upon me to bring it to you without delay."

It was mid-August when Captain Pennan returned to Plymouth, and more than a month passed before he came again, an inexplicable delay which did nothing to set Charity's mind at ease. To Ellen she made light of her misgivings, finding a dozen reasons to account for Tom's failure to bring them news of Sarah, but in her heart she believed none of them.

These anxieties were made no easier to bear by her ever-present fears for Darrell's safety, for in those latter months of 1650 tension in the West Country was steadily mounting. Travellers there were frequently stopped and questioned, for an outbreak of rebellion at Weymouth and Portland in July had made the authorities doubly aware of the dangerous currents which stirred and simmered among the outwardly subjugated followers of the King. To be discovered giving shelter to Royalist agents, or to be concerned, however remotely, in any kind of seditious activity was to run the risk of imprisonment, yet local leaders in every part of the West, Darrell among them, continued to muster their forces and prepare the way for the rising they believed must surely come when King Charles led a Scottish army into England. But the Scots tarried beyond the Border, treating their King little better than a prisoner, while Cromwell turned his back upon the carnage in Ireland and came hastening home to face the new challenge. The English Royalists hesitated, reluctant to trust the hated Scots, and only in the West Country was there any effective organisation.

At last, on a misty September day, Tom Pennan

came riding again to the Moat House, but the news he bore brought little reassurance. He greeted Charity's eager questions with a frown.

"That is a strange household, Miss Charity," he told her bluntly. "On my first visit I was greeted by Mrs Dallett, Taynton's sister, and told that Mrs Taynton was indisposed. I replied that since I had been charged to deliver messages to the lady herself, I would return another day. My second visit followed the same pattern as the first, save that this time I was told that Taynton and his wife had gone to visit friends."

By this time Charity, too, was frowning, and as Tom paused she asked frankly: "Do you suppose, sir, that Sarah was being deliberately kept from you?"

"That suspicion did cross my mind," he admitted, "and since my curiosity had by now been aroused I determined to see her in spite of them. I paid four more visits to the house, and in the end they wearied of my persistence and I was admitted to Mrs Taynton's presence."

"Well, sir?" Charity prompted impatiently as he hesitated. "How looked my cousin? What said she?"

"She said everything was proper!" Tom's voice was noncommittal. "That she was pleased to renew our acquaintance and regretted that she had not been able to receive me on my previous visits. That she had heard I had suffered some misfortune on my last voyage, and wished me a speedy return to full health. When I told her that you and Ellen were disturbed because you had received no word from her, she said merely that her brother visited her whenever he was in Plymouth, and that she supposed you to have had news of her from him, as she had had news of you." He paused, and then added in his driest tone: "Of course, Mrs Dallett and Miss Catherine Taynton were present all this while."

Charity looked sharply at him. "You think that Sarah might have spoken differently had you been alone?"

He shrugged. "How can I tell? From my previous acquaintance with her I remember your cousin as a merry creature with laughter never far from her lips. Now she is pale and quiet and oddly subdued, though it may be merely that the responsibilities of marriage weigh heavily upon her. With Taynton's sister in the house, and four step-daughters of whom the youngest is barely ten years her junior, she must be beset by difficulties."

"Yes, that is true!" Charity agreed with a sigh. "Mr Taynton's daughters may well resent a young girl like Sarah taking their mother's place, and if they show dislike of her it would wound her deeply, just as the hostility of the people here wounded her. Sarah's is a nature which craves affection." She was silent for a moment, and then added abruptly, "What of Mr Taynton himself?"

"I have not seen him since my return, but my brothers tell me that he is deeply immersed in business, and in the affairs of the city. He was in London in the spring, and stayed for several weeks with his brother there. Rumour has it that the affairs of the Taynton family prosper exceedingly under our present masters."

Charity received this information in silence, aware once again, beyond her immediate concern for Sarah, of the conviction that Taynton's connection with Jonas embodied a threat to Darrell's safety. Tom watched her for a few moments, observing the frown between her brows, and the trouble in her eyes, and at length said quietly,

"I wish I could have brought you happier tidings of your cousin, Miss Charity, for I have something else to tell which cannot fail to dismay you, as it must dismay all loyal subjects of the King. On the third of this month, at Dunbar on the east coast of Scotland, the Scottish army suffered a grievous defeat at Cromwell's hands."

"Another defeat!" Charity sank down on a stool, staring at Tom in dismay. "God's mercy! Is the man indeed invincible?"

"It would seem so," he agreed dispiritedly. "As I heard it, three thousand Scottish soldiers were slain, and another nine thousand fell prisoner to the Roundheads."

"Is this then the end of all hope of deliverance by the Scots?"

"Who can tell? The alliance could never be popular among Royalists in England, but at least it provided an army to fight for the Crown. We can but wait and hope, Miss Charity, for the future is in God's hands."

Wait and hope they did, throughout the whole of the autumn and winter, though there was little enough for hope to feed upon. The Scots did indeed rally their shattered army, and King Charles II was duly crowned at Scone, but there was ill news in plenty to offset these hopeful tidings. In October, William of Orange died, and with him died all hope of support from Holland. In November and December a premature rising of Royalists in Norfolk ended in disaster, with a score of executions and the imprisonment of leaders in several other areas. The arrest of two prominent Royalists in Hampshire struck a shrewd blow at the Western Association, but though the hope of a successful rising in the West seemed to be fading, the organisation itself survived, kept alive by the enthusiasm of those who had created it.

All this news reached Charity piecemeal, sometimes from Tom, who continued to visit the Moat House undeterred by Jonas's black looks, and sometimes from Darrell, though as the winter closed in her meetings with him became ever more difficult to arrange. She was conscious always of Daniel Stotewood's baleful presence; of his pale eyes watching her; of his lanky figure lurking stealthily in the background as she went about her daily tasks, and this constant, furtive spying wrought her nerves to a screaming point. Had she thought it would do the least good she would have complained to Jonas or her aunt, but for all she knew the man might be acting upon their orders.

One thing only gave Charity and Ellen any satisfaction, and that was the fact that at last they had received word from Sarah. Prompted perhaps by Tom's persistence and unwilling to suffer from it again, Jonas and Taynton had apparently decided that she should be allowed to write to Ellen from time to time. The first of these letters was brought by Jonas when he returned from a visit to Plymouth in November, and Ellen hastened at once to the nursery to tell Charity about it.

"I could scarcely believe it when Jonas told me that he had brought it," she said breathlessly. "Oh, Charity, Sarah is with child, and expects to be brought to bed at the end of April. I am so glad! When she has a babe to love she will perhaps be less cast down by the unfriendliness of her step-daughters and their aunt."

Charity took the letter and read it, and a little frown creased her brow. It seemed well enough, with its news of the coming child, questions about Ellen's own family, and loving greetings to Charity herself, and yet, as she read it, she was aware of something strangely lacking. These stiff, formal phrases conjured up no picture of Sarah herself, and Charity felt certain that Edward Taynton or his sister had directed every word.

### III

On the first day of March, Charity stood at the nursery window and looked out upon a bleak and colourness landscape where the sullen grip of winter still lay heavily. The trees in the garden lifted bare branches to the cold, grey sky, and in the flower-beds beneath them not the smallest spear of green was yet visible. As Charity regarded the cheerless scene her heart felt as cold and lifeless as the garden, her spirits as heavy as the clouds which hung above it. Two years had passed since Charles I died beneath the executioner's axe, and in spite of all the perilous work done, and all the dangers dared, deliverance, both for England and for herself, seemed as far off as it had done upon that bitter day.

She turned with a start as Polly came into the room. The maidservant appeared to be labouring under some strong emotion, and informed her that Mrs Shenfield wanted to see Miss Charity at once in the parlour. Daniel Stotewood, she added, had just arrived from Plymouth with letters from his master.

Puzzled and more than a little perturbed, Charity

hurried downstairs and found Elizabeth sitting by the parlour fire. A letter lay in her lap, and her fingers tapped restlessly against it as she sat frowning before her, but when Charity entered the room she looked round and beckoned her nearer.

"Stotewood brings ill news from Plymouth!" she said abruptly. "Your cousin Sarah was brought to bed two days ago."

Charity stared at her in dismay. "So soon? 'Tis a full two months to her time!" She broke off, looking at her aunt with sharp foreboding. "The child . . . ?"

"Stillborn!" Mrs Shenfield replied curtly. "The ways of the Lord are strange indeed, for 'twas a boy, the son Mr Taynton so ardently desired. Sarah lies grievously ill, and Jonas bids me send you to Plymouth to nurse her."

"I?" Charity exclaimed in blank astonishment. "Are there none in her husband's house to care for her?"

"Curb your pert tongue, mistress! Are you reluctant to go to Sarah in her need and her distress?"

"You know that I am not! If I can help her I will go gladly."

"You will go, my girl, gladly or not!" Elizabeth informed her grimly. "The hour is too late for you to set forth today, but make yourself ready to start tomorrow at first light. Stotewood will be your escort and your guide."

This information gave Charity no pleasure at all, but she knew that it would be useless to protest. Her anxiety for Sarah, and her pity for her in this new sorrow, were profound, and yet a tiny doubt lurked at the back of her mind. As she made her preparations a question, so nebulous that she could scarcely have

144

put it into words, fretted at the edge of consciousness, asking what deeper reason lay behind this urgent summons. She wished fervently that she could consult Darrell, but no opportunity occurred to visit the Dower House, and she had to content herself with writing to him, and giving the letter to Polly to deliver after her departure.

Next day, in the first grey light of a wintry morning, she found herself riding across the park with Daniel Stotewood beside her. She was profoundly thankful that two horses had been provided, for she had feared that she might be expected to ride pillion behind her detested companion, a common method of travel for women of all classes. That, at least, she had been spared.

They passed through the village at a brisk trot which gave her no chance to do more than nod and smile at the few people they encountered, and, crossing the river, set their faces towards Plymouth. For the most part they rode in silence, their whole attention occupied in avoiding the hazards of the narrow, ill-kept road which still bore many signs of the ravages of winter. Great puddles many feet across hid in their depths unsuspected pitfalls of deep holes or treacherous stones; there were stretches of mud through which the horses' hooves squelched laboriously; huge branches torn down by the winter gales were left to rot where they had fallen. It was bitterly cold, and Charity huddled closer into her thick, hooded cloak, her gloved fingers numb and stiff upon her horse's bridle.

She had not been farther afield than the village for years, and never in her life as far as Plymouth, and had the occasion for the journey been different, and her companion more congenial, might have felt some interest or excitement in spite of the weather. As it was, she could only wish earnestly for the journey to be over, for even the prospect of being thrust into a strange and probably hostile household seemed preferable to her present situation.

Their progress was slow and the morning already well advanced when, with several miles still before them, the rain which had been threatening since dawn began in earnest. For a little while they rode on, bending their heads and hunching their shoulders against the icy lash of it, and then Stotewood pointed to a group of tumbledown buildings a short distance from the roadside and said curtly:

"Yonder is shelter o' sorts! We'd best bide there till the worst of this be past."

Charity nodded, and urged her horse after his as he turned in the direction of the buildings. When they reached them she saw that this had once been a small farmstead, and had obviously been the scene of a skirmish between Cavalier and Roundhead, for both the house and its outbuildings bore the signs of battle and had been partially destroyed by fire. Enough remained, however, of blackened walls and sagging roof to give a measure of protection from the wind and rain, and she slipped thankfully from the saddle and stepped into the makeshift shelter, while Stotewood led the horses in after her and tethered them to a pile of broken timbers.

Charity, stiff with cold and from the unaccustomed hours in the saddle, began to pace up and down the confined space, trying to restore some warmth to her limbs. From time to time she glanced anxiously through

the broken doorway at the rain which still beat piti-
lessly, with no sign of abating, across the desolate
scene beyond, for the situation was beginning to make
her feel uneasy. The loneliness of this ruined home-
stead, the constant hiss and drip of the rain, the grey
and cheerless landscape were all infinitely depressing,
and she was acutely aware of Daniel Stotewood leaning against the wall nearby, his eyes following every
move she made, his silence more oppressive than his
customary denunciations and prophecies of damnation.
At last, to break a silence which was becoming intolerable, she asked:

"How much farther to Plymouth?"

"Two or three miles," he replied brusquely, and
Charity frowned again at the beating rain.

"Perhaps it would be better to ride on despite the
weather. This rain may go on all day, and before long
the roads will be impassable."

He wrapped his heavy cloak closer about his lanky
form and said laconically, "We'll bide!"

The insolence of his manner, even more than the
words themselves, roused Charity to sudden anger.
She swung more fully to face him, saying imperiously:
"I have decided to ride on! I am in haste to reach my
cousin, and would rather journey through the rain than
tarry in this dreary place. Bring the horses, and let
us begone."

Stotewood made no attempt to obey her. Straighten-
ing from his lounging position against the wall, so that
he stood between her and the horses, he said harshly:
"Woman, be warned! It is not fitting for the ungodly
to defy the righteous, and in this place, vanity and
sinful pride will avail you little."

Charity stared at him, her previous misgivings now wholly swallowed by anger, and then she stepped forward so that only a yard or so separated her from him. "Do you dare to threaten me, sirrah?" she said in a voice of cold disdain. "I have endured a surfeit of your canting insolence of late, and so, I fancy, has my kinsman, your master. You would do well to think less of your vaunted godliness and more of your duty to the family you are paid to serve. I say we shall ride on, and at once!"

She put out her hand to thrust him from her path, but he caught her by the wrist, and then seized her other hand as she lifted it to strike him. The bony fingers held her with a strength against which her efforts to free herself were of no avail, and now alarm pierced her again, more sharply than before.

"Terrible shall be the wrath of the Lord against those who mock and defy Him," he raved, "for they shall be enmeshed in their own evil and cast into eternal darkness! Their pride shall be flung down, and their lusts consumed in the fires of hell." His hold on her wrists tightened painfully and he jerked her towards him, his gaunt face now close to hers. "Only in humiliation shall humility be learned, and the sins and the shame be purged by suffering."

For a few seconds Charity stared, fascinated, into the glittering eyes which seemed to bore into her own, and as she stared, saw a baser passion kindle behind the religious frenzy, sensed a subtle change in the way he was holding her. A surge of fear and disgust lent her strength and she wrenched herself free, thrusting him away with such vigour that he slipped and measured his length on the muddy ground. Before he could rise she had reached the horses, and snatched from its place on his saddle the pistol carried as a protection against the dangers of the road. Stotewood, scrambling to his feet to plunge in pursuit, found himself confronted by it and halted in dismay.

"One step nearer and I put a pistol-ball through your leg," Charity warned him, and though her voice was trembling, the hand which held the weapon was not. "Do not suppose I could not do so. I was taught when scarcely more than a child to handle a weapon such as this."

Her words and manner, and above all, the unwavering barrel of the pistol, convinced Stotewood of the folly of disregarding them. He stood glaring at her, his hands clenching spasmodically as though he would have liked to feel them around her throat, while Charity studied him with the utmost contempt. Finally she said:

"Draw back from me! Back, I say!"

She waited until he had retreated as far as the confined space allowed, and then with her free hand unhitched the horses and, using the timbers as a mounting-block, climbed nimbly into the saddle. Then, motioning him to precede her from the building, she followed with the horses, ducking her head beneath the low doorway. Outside, she reined back and nodded towards the second horse.

"Mount," she ordered curtly, "and ride before me! Be sure that I shall not put up this pistol until we reach Plymouth, nor shall I hesitate to use it if you give me cause."

In sullen silence he obeyed her, and the horses plodded forward through the driving rain. The few remaining miles of that eventful journey seemed interminable to Charity, for she dared not relax her vigilance, while the weather and the appalling state of the road added to her difficulties. At least they found themselves threading the narrow streets of the town and finally, to her intense relief, Stotewood drew rein before a tall, imposing house with upper storeys overhanging the street, and, turning in the saddle, said abruptly:

"This be Taynton's house."

Charity slid wearily from the saddle and stumbled up two or three steps to hammer on the door, while Stotewood stood holding the horses' bridles and watching her with venomous fury. When the door opened, Charity turned to look at him.

"Come within," she said curtly. "Mr. Taynton shall learn how ill you have discharged your errand."

It was not Edward Taynton, however, who met them inside the house, but Jonas himself. He was standing before a roaring fire in the panelled room to which they were led, talking to a thin, middle-aged woman in widow's weeds who was obviously Taynton's sister.

"So, cousin!" he greeted Charity. "You are come as I bade you!"

Charity went slowly forward. She was drenched and exhausted and chilled to the bone, but she kept her head high and even met his eyes with a glimmer of the customary mockery in her own.

"I am happy to find you here, Jonas," she said quietly, "since it gives me an opportunity to tell you that your lackey here, for all his professions of godliness, is of as carnel a turn of mind as other men. For the latter part of our journey I was obliged to hold him at bay with this."

She took the pistol from beneath her cloak and laid it on the table. Jonas, who had listened to her with a gathering frown, looked at it and then at Daniel Stotewood, now standing just inside the room. For a long moment his master regarded him without speaking, his expression revealing nothing, and then he turned to the woman seated beside the fire.

"Mrs Dallet, my kinswoman will need food and dry clothes before she takes up her duties!" His voice was as expressionless as his look. "Will you be good enough to see that she is furnished with them?"

The widow inclined her head in assent and got up, signing to Charity to follow her. It seemed that she was as taciturn as her brother, to whom she bore also a strong physical resemblance, and Charity did not find her prepossessing.

Not until the door had closed behind the two women did Jonas move. Then he walked deliberately across the room to Stotewood and dealt him a buffet on the side of the head which sent him reeling against the wall.

"Fool!" Jonas spoke between his teeth, in a voice harsh with fury. "Impatient fool! I warn you, Stotewood, if all goes awry because of your bungling, it will go hard with you. I have not waited and schemed for so long only to have *you* overset my plans!"

# 9

SARAH was indeed gravely ill, so ill that for several days after Charity's arrival she seemed scarcely aware of her cousin's presence. Charity nursed her devotedly, shocked and alarmed by the change she saw in her, and occupied the few spare minutes left to her in endeavouring to form an accurate opinion of the household.

She did not see Edward Taynton himself until the morning after her arrival, when he came to the sickroom for a few minutes. He greeted her with curt civility and asked a number of questions concerning Sarah's progress, but Charity was left with an impression of cold detachment. Mr Taynton's mind was obviously occupied by weightier matters than the health of his young wife.

The women of the family she found even less likeable than the master of the house. Mrs Dallett was opinionated and overbearing, and made it plain from the outset that she resented Charity's inclusion in the household, for she went out of her way to belittle everything the younger woman did and to contradict on every possible occasion such orders as she gave to the servants. Charity suspected that she had behaved in the same way to Sarah, but if this were so, Mrs Dallett found that she had a very different person to deal with now, for though Charity was unfailingly courteous she refused to be intimidated.

The four daughters of the house, Catherine, Mary, Prudence and Jane, ranged in age from nine to fifteen, but during the first few days it was only with the eldest, Catherine, that Charity had much contact. Catherine, was a tall, thin, ungainly girl with the same large features and nondescript colouring as her father, and a manner so quiet that it verged on the secretive. She was civil enough, but there was a slyness about her which Charity found repellent.

Sarah's condition slowly improved, but though her strength increased she remained unresponsive to all that was done for her, even Charity's loving care seeming to make no impression upon her. It was as though she had withdrawn behind a barrier deliberately raised against the rest of the world, and Charity, supposing this to be reaction from the shock and grief of losing her first child, could only hope that as time went by she would recover something of her former spirits.

A week or so after her arrival in Plymouth she was going towards Sarah's room when she saw Catherine Taynton emerging from it. The girl slipped quietly past her with demure face and downcast eyes, but when Charity entered the room she found Sarah prone upon her pillows, sobbing bitterly. Charity hurried forward in dismay and sat down beside her on the bed, gathering the frail figure into her arms, and Sarah, turning to that loving embrace, clung to her with the first real feeling she had shown.

"Sarah, my dearest, hush! You will do yourself some harm!" Charity rocked gently to and fro, trying to soothe the wild sobs which were shaking Sarah's whole body. "What has Catherine been saying to you? My dear little cousin, tell me!"

At first there was no response save an even more desperate weeping, but at length Sarah murmured something almost completely unintelligible. Charity, able to make out only some reference to the baby, held her closer and whispered the only comfort she could think of.

"Dear, it is a bitter grief to you, but you must trust in the infinite mercy and wisdom of God. This babe was taken from you, but there will be others—"

"No!" The denial came sharp and clear as Sarah raised her head from Charity's shoulder. "I pray constantly that I shall never bear another child! I am thankful that my baby died, and if God were truly merciful I should have died, too!"

"Sarah!" Not all Charity's efforts could keep the shocked dismay from her voice. "You are beside yourself, and know not what you say."

"Do I not?" There was a world of bitterness in Sarah's trembling voice and tear-drenched blue eyes. "What joy could lie in bringing a babe into this house, where it would be hated as its mother is hated? I have known more wretchedness here than I ever dreamed was possible, and the only instance of Divine mercy I have known since my marriage is that my son was spared the unhappiness I have endured."

"Sarah, you are quite distraught!" Charity spoke in gentle rebuke, smoothing back the fair curls which clung damply to the girl's forehead. "This is a cheerless house, I know, but no one in it hates you. That is an idle fancy born of sickness and sorrow."

"They all hate me, and they all have their reasons." Sarah freed herself from Charity's embrace and lay back wearily against the tumbled pillows. Her indrawn breath shuddered in a sob, but her voice was flat now with the calmness of despair and carried far greater conviction than her previous hysteria. "The younger girls are urged on by their aunt to hate me because I have taken their mother's place. Mrs Dallett hates me because she has a son whom she hopes will inherit part of the Taynton fortune, and she sees in me, and the children I may bear, a threat to that ambition. And Catherine?" She paused, and gave a little, mirthless laugh that choked into another sob. "Catherine hates me more than any of them because she is jealous."

Charity opened her lips to protest, but then paused, for this, at least, seemed likely enough. Catherine, so awkward and plain, could very well be consumed by jealousy of the pretty, sweet-natured girl who had become her stepmother.

"There is a young man who comes sometimes to this house," Sarah's sad, weary voice went on. "He is the son of one of my husband's friends, and it is understood between the two families that he and Catherine will shortly marry. When I first came to Plymouth he conceived an admiration for me, and Catherine discovered it. She said nothing to me—that is not her way—but she waited and schemed until she could make it appear to her father that the fault was mine, that I had provoked the boy to this folly. He would believe none of my denials, and he was so angry . . ." She broke off, shuddering and pressing the back of one hand against her lips.

Charity reached out and took the other hand between her own. She was overwhelmed by dismay, and a deep, futile anger against those who had transformed merry, high-spirited Sarah into this pitiful, frightened ghost of her former self.

"Angry he may have been, my dear," she said after a moment, "but do not think, surely, that your husband hates you?"

"No, he does not hate me," Sarah replied drearily, "neither does he love me. I mean nothing to him at all. He married me for one reason only—to give him a son to inherit the wealth he spends his life amassing —and now I have failed him in that. Catherine was taunting me with that failure just before you came in, for all the household knows how bitterly my husband now regards me." She drew a long, quivering breath. "Did you know that the first words he spoke to me after the child was born were words of cruel reproach?"

She paused again, but this time Charity made no reply, for in the face of these starkly related facts she could find no comfort to give. Sarah's voice was weak now with exhaustion, but it was plain that this chance to unburden herself at last of her bitterness and grief was in itself a kind of healing.

"I have tried to be a good wife," she resumed wretchedly after a moment. "When Hal deserted me in my time of greatest need, when I realised how worthless had been all his declarations of love, I resolved that in the marriage arranged for me I would do my best to be dutiful and faithful, and care well for my husband even though I could not love him, but these resolutions I have been given no chance to keep. Mrs Dallett refuses to yield up to me the ordering of the household, the girls join together to plague me, and if I complain of their conduct to Taynton they always contrive to make me appear in the wrong. He has many cares and responsibilities, and greatly dislikes to be vexed with domestic troubles." She closed her eyes, but from beneath her lashes the tears began once more to creep slowly down her white cheeks. "Perhaps this unhappiness is the punishment which Jonas and my mother prophesied for me! When I defied them in the matter of my marriage, they warned me that God would punish me for my wickedness."

"Child, you were guilty of no wickedness!" Charity said gently. "Of folly, perhaps, but nothing more."

"Folly, indeed!" Sarah spoke without opening her eyes, but her voice was charged with bitterness. "Only a fool would have believed, as I did, in vows of constancy as false as him who made them."

Charity sat looking at her with troubled eyes, wondering whether it would comfort Sarah, or distress her even more, to know that Hal had not deceived her, but had forsaken her only because of demands of duty and loyalty which transcended even the promises he had made to her. It was a question which could not be answered, for it would be impossible to tell Sarah the truth without disclosing also the existence of a conspiracy, and that Charity knew she had no right to do.

II

During the weeks which followed, Charity realised that what Sarah had told her was true. Edward Tayn-

157

ton was away from the house a great deal, and when he was at home spent most of his time in his study, paying little heed, unless something occurred to disturb him, to what the female members of his family were doing. Mrs Dallett and Catherine were therefore able to do very much as they liked, and contrived, in a subtle way which was very difficult to combat, to set Sarah and Charity apart as though they were intruders with no right to be in the household at all. Catherine, in particular, had an unpleasant talent for mischief-making, and since she was by far the most forceful, as well as the eldest of the four sisters, the younger girls faithfully followed her example.

Had Charity herself been in Sarah's place she would have given them short shrift, but though there were many occasions when she was tempted to bring matters to a head, she was restrained by the thought that her cousin might suffer for it when she herself had returned to the Moat House. Sarah's welfare must be her foremost consideration, and though Charity was desperately anxious about Darrell, and fretted at being so completely cut off from him at a time when the Royalist conspiracies must surely be reaching a climax, she worried also at the prospect of leaving Sarah alone again in this unfriendly household. The girl was slowly regaining a measure of physical strength, but there was a listlessness about her, an apathy from which nothing seemed to rouse her, which Charity found infinitely disturbing.

When she had been in Plymouth for a little more than a month, and Sarah was strong enough to be up and about again, Jonas came to pay them a visit. Charity immediately supposed that this presaged her own return to the Moat House, but to her surprise he made no mention of this, and when she tentatively broached the subject herself, merely turned a sardonic glance upon her.

"I well know, cousin, that you are eager to return to Conyngton St John," he said mockingly, "but you must curb your impatience while your presence is still required here. Is that not so, Sarah? Can you yet spare Charity to us?"

"Her presence is a great comfort to me!" His sister, flustered by the unexpected question, stumbled piteously in her reply. "I would have her stay, but if she is needed at home—"

"The Moat House can contrive without her for the present," he said carelessly. "She may remain with you as long as you have need of her."

Charity said no more, but once again she was conscious of an inward stirring of uneasiness, a presentiment of trouble, for she found something decidedly sinister in Jonas's belated concern for his sister's pleasure. For some reason of his own he wished to keep Charity away from Darrell, and though he might be prompted by mere spite, she had an uncomfortable conviction that this was not so. A sense of utter helplessness took possession of her, for here in Plymouth, far away from everyone upon whose friendship she could depend, she knew that she was more completely at Jonas's mercy than she could ever be at the Moat House.

Yet there was one friend whom she had for the moment forgotten, but who had not, it seemed, forgotten her. During the second week of April, Tom Pennan arrived at the house, making the excuse that he was leaving Plymouth next day to visit his sister Ellen, and had come to inquire whether Charity or Sarah wished him to carry letters to her.

"The time draws near when I must put to sea again," he explained, "and I have promised Ellen that I will spend some time with her before I go. I am expected at the Moat House tomorrow, but I will be happy to fetch such letters on my way out of the town, and carry them with me."

His words had ostensibly been addressed to Sarah, since both Catherine and Mary Taynton were in the room, but Charity, looking up to meet his eyes, knew that he was offering to bear news not only to the Moat House but also to Darrell, and was conscious of a surge of gratitude. She said quietly:

"For my part, Captain Pennan, I shall be happy to avail myself of your generosity, and Sarah, I am sure, will do likewise."

Sarah murmured agreement, though without much enthusiasm, and Tom, after spending a short while with them, took his leave, promising to return next morning for the letters. That night Charity sat up long after the rest of the household had retired, pouring into a letter to Darrell all her love and her doubts, her anxiety for Sarah and her fears for his own safety. She had already written briefly to Ellen, and urged Sarah into doing likewise and into penning a note to her mother, and next morning, taking all four letters with her, she kept watch for Tom and waylaid him as soon as he was admitted to the house. Dismissing the servant, she silently handed Tom the letters with the one addressed to Darrell uppermost. He glanced at it, and then looked at her with a smile.

"You may trust me to bear it safely, Miss Charity," he assured her in a low voice, then, stowing the letters away, added abruptly, "How long do you remain in Plymouth?"

She sighed. "I would give much to know. Jonas pretends that I am still needed here, but Sarah no longer has need of nursing, and since it has never been his custom to consider her feelings, he must have some other reason. Mayhap it is no more than malice, but I will own I am uneasy."

Tom nodded. "I, too, would trust Shenfield least when he shows concern for others, but perhaps, as you say, it is no more than petty spite. If you are still in Plymouth when I return, I will endeavour to bring an answer to your letter." He broke off as Mrs Dallet emerged from a room nearby, and then added more loudly: "I will tell my sister what you say, Miss Charity. My compliments to Mrs Taynton and the young ladies."

He bowed to Mrs Dallet, took leave of Charity and departed, while Charity herself rejoined Sarah, feeling a little comforted by the thought that her letter would almost certainly be in Darrell's hands before nightfall. Like Tom, she distrusted Jonas most of all in his present obliging mood, and was thankful that an opportunity had occurred to put Darrell on his guard against the possibility of some move against him.

A week went by uneventfully. A spell of fine, mild spring weather had set in, and Charity persuaded Sarah to venture out of doors. At first she would go no further than the small, walled garden behind the house, but Charity persisted until she had been coaxed to walk with her, a manservant in attendance, for a short way through the neighbouring streets.

While the fine weather lasted these walks became a daily occurrence, and one afternoon, when they had returned to the house and Charity had left Sarah to rest for a while, a servant came seeking her with the news that a messenger had just arrived from her cousin, Lady Linslade, and was asking for her. Charity stared at the man in astonishment.

"From Lady Linslade? Are you certain?"

"That I am! The man said her ladyship do have heard o' Mrs Taynton's illness and sent him to ask how she does. He be in the parlour."

"I will see him." Charity waved the servant away and went quickly towards the parlour, a frown creasing her brow. It was quite possible that the Linslades had heard from Darrell that Sarah had been ill, but it was odd that Beth should direct a message to her rather than to Edward Taynton or to Sarah herself.

When she reached the parlour she found a slight young man, plainly and somewhat shabbily dressed, standing looking from the window, his back to the room. She stared at him, her frown deepening, and then said rather sharply:

"I am Charity Shenfield! What do you want with me?"

Slowly the man turned to face her, and the incredible suspicion which had dawned with her first sight of him crystallised into astounded certainty. In spite of shabby clothes, and the small, pointed beard which subtly altered the shape of his face, the visitor was instantly recognisable as Henry Mordisford.

Charity shut the door rather quickly and stood leaning against it, staring at Hal while he looked back at her with a curious mingling of amusement, apology and defiance in his eyes. Then, recovering herself a little, she moved hurriedly towards him, saying in a whisper:

"Mr Mordisford, are you mad? In the name of heaven, what do you here?"

He shook his head. "No harm, Miss Charity, upon my word, but first I must tell you that I am one John Sedgeworth whose family lives near Dorringford. I am in Plymouth on a matter of business for my father, and Lady Linslade asked me to seek news of her sister. Will you remember that?" She nodded, not understanding but realising that argument would be both futile and dangerous. Hal took a letter from the breast of his doublet and thrust it into her hand. "Hide that, and read it only when you can be sure no one is by. It is from Darrell."

Charity paused in the act of putting the letter in her pocket to stare at him in renewed astonishment. "Darrell knows that you are here?"

"It is at his behest, in part at least, that I have come. I will explain in a moment, but first—is it likely that we can be overheard?"

"No, I think not!" Charity pressed a hand to her brow, trying to think clearly. "Mr Taynton is not at home, and Mrs Dallett and Catherine have gone to visit a neighbour. The younger girls are in the schoolroom. Wait!" She went quickly to the door, opened it to glance to right and left, and then shut it again and returned to Hal. "The servants, I think, are all occupied elsewhere, but speak softly, sir, I pray you. What has happened?"

A look of the utmost bitterness came into his eyes. "In a word, Miss Charity, disaster! Last month a Royalist agent, Isaac Birkenhead, was arrested at Greenock as he embarked for the Isle of Man. His papers were seized, and the cowardly wretch turned informer to save himself. The whole conspiracy in the North-west was wrecked, and his disclosures also put the authorities on the track of a second agent, Thomas Coke, who was taken in London at the end of March. He also purchased his life by betraying those who had trusted him. There have been arrests beyond number! The Presbyterians in London, Royalists in Kent and many of our own supporters in the South and West. Believe me, Miss Charity, between them those two foul traitors have destroyed the work of the past two years and shattered Royalist hopes in England. Even if the King marches south, there can be no rising now to support him."

Charity turned blindly to a bench which stood against the wall nearby and sank down upon it, for she was trembling so violently that she feared her limbs would no longer support her. After a moment, in a voice which sounded strangely unlike her own, she managed to ask the question which had leapt terribly to the forefront of her mind.

"Darrell? Dear God! Mr Mordisford, they have not arrested him?"

"No, no! I believe he is in no immediate danger, but as we well know, your kinsman is already suspicious and will spare no effort to prove him guilty of sedition. That is one reason why I have come to you today. Darrell believes that he can do no more in England, and that with your cousin so determined to destroy him it is no longer safe for either of you to tarry. He is resolved that you shall both seek safety overseas without delay."

She stared at him, torn between dismay and gladness. "But Conyngton? If Darrell goes into exile, Jonas will surely find a way to secure it for himself."

"He will secure it even more surely if Darrell is executed for treason," Hal pointed out ruthlessly, "and what would become of *you* then? Miss Charity, I am but the messenger. The reasons in favour of flight Darrell has set forth in his letter, but one thing he bade me say to you. "Tell her," he said, "that the time for argument is past and the decision taken. The time has come for her to keep the promise she has made to me.' "

A fleeting smile touched Charity's lips. "Does he think me reluctant to do so, that he sends so peremptory a command? Yet how can such flight be accomplished?"

"If you can win free of this house without arousing suspicion, it may be done. There is a fishing village a few miles along the coast which I and other Royalist agents have used more than once, and where there are secure places to hide until the wind favours a crossing to France. Darrell will meet us there."

"Where is he now?"

"He bides at Conyngton until tomorrow, and then goes to meet Linslade and some others. After that he will join us at the village I spoke of."

"If he is still free to do so! God's mercy! What madness prompts a meeting at such a time?"

"It had already been agreed upon, though for a happier purpose. I was to meet with my Lord Beauchamp in London and bear his commands to certain groups of Royalists in the West, but when I reached London I learned that Beauchamp was already in the Tower and our whole organisation in ruins. There was nothing left for me to do but escape while I might and ride westward hearing news of disaster instead of tidings of hope. After I had talked with Darrell it was decided that while he went to meet his friends and warn them what has befallen, I should come to you, since it would not be possible for *him* to visit this house."

"It is dangerous for *you* to be here, sir," Charity said seriously. "What if you were recognised?"

He shrugged. "I knew that Shenfield is at the Moat House, and there is no one here save yourself who knows my face."

"Except Sarah!" Charity added quietly. "You came hoping to see her, did you not?"

He shook his head. "I came determined to see her," he corrected calmly, "but first I had to discharge my errand to you. I have done so faithfully, so now, I pray you, fetch Sarah to me."

Charity faced him squarely. "To what purpose, my friend? I will not be the means of causing her more unhappiness."

"Do you think *me* less careful of her happiness than yourself? I will be frank with you, Miss Charity! If Sarah will come, I mean to take her with me to France."

She frowned. "Sir, she is Edward Taynton's wife!"

"I know it, but I know, too, how unworthy he is to be her husband. When you wrote to Darrell you made no secret of the trials she has had to bear, and he showed me those parts of your letter which concerned Sarah. This is our only chance to find happiness together! It may be months, even years, before I may venture to set foot in England again."

She regarded him with troubled eyes. "Sarah believes that you deserted her in her hour of need. She is very bitter towards you."

"Let me but see her, and I will convince her it was not so. For the love of pity, Miss Charity, do as I ask!"

Charity hesitated, her heart prompting her to yield to his entreaties, her practical mind acknowledging the folly of doing so; and while she hesitated, the decision was mercifully taken from her. The door opened and Sarah herself came into the room, saying eagerly:

"Charity, it is indeed true that a messenger has come from Beth? How did she . . . ?"

She broke off, for she was now fully into the room and had a clear view of the supposed messenger. She stood staring, every vestige of colour draining from her face, while Charity, fearing that she might make some outcry, moved quickly towards her. She had barely reached her when without a sound Sarah collapsed, and would have fallen but for her cousin's supporting arms.

Hal sprang forward, and Charity let him take Sarah from her while she herself went quickly to the open door. A cautious glance outside assured her that there was no one within earshot, and, closing the door firmly, she went back to where Hal had set Sarah down in the chair by the fire. The girl was already recovering her senses, and Charity thrust Hal aside and bent over her as she opened her eyes.

"Charity!" she said in a faint, puzzled voice. "What happened?" Then her glance went past the other woman and her eyes widened. She said in an incredulous whisper: " Hal!"

"Sarah!" Charity spoke sharply, in a voice as muted as her cousin's. "In God's name, make no outcry!"

Sarah looked at her for a moment, and then her gaze returned to Hal. She was still deathly pale, but now the first shock was passing and bitterness and resentment taking the place of stupefaction. In a low voice charged with anger and scorn, she said:

"Why are you here? Do you not know that you come nearly two years too late?"

"Sarah!' Hal dropped to one knee beside the chair and caught her hands in his, holding them fast in spite of her efforts to pull them away. "I swear before God that I did not willingly forsake you! When I came to Devon just before your marriage I was upon a mission for the King, to whom I had pledged unreservedly my honour and my service. My life was not then mine to do with as I willed, to risk, even for your dear sake." He paused, his gaze anxiously searching her face, seeing doubt replacing the bitterness in her eyes, and then he added pleadingly: "My dearest love, will you not trust me, now that I have entrusted *you* with knowledge which imperils not merely my own safety, but the safety and happiness of your cousin and of Darrell Conyngton also?"

She continued to stare at him in silence, and then her gaze turned towards Charity, entreating confirmation of his words. In a low voice, Charity gave it.

"Sarah, this is the truth! It was too perilous a secret to tell you then, and may God protect us all if you are careless of it now!"

"Now?" Sarah's puzzled, pleading eyes looked from one to the other. "I do not understand! Hal, why are you here?"

"Because I am forced to leave England again, this time with scant hope of return," he replied simply, "and I could not go, my love, without seeing you again."

"Hal!" Sarah's voice trembled with desperate entreaty. "Oh, Hal, take me with you! I have been so unhappy!"

Charity turned away from them and stood looking from the window into the narrow street. Her thoughts were a turmoil of excitement, misgiving, and a gladness which in spite of everything could not be denied. She and Darrell could be together at last. The remorseless march of events had taken the decision out of their hands, and though it would tear her heart to leave Conyngton, and her friends there, to Jonas's doubtful mercy, flight could no longer be accounted a betrayal.

Yet there were many risks still to be taken before they could win free, and at any moment their privacy might be invaded by some member of the Taynton household. Spurred by that thought, she turned to face Sarah and Hal.

"Our plans must be made without delay," she said, quietly. "You said, sir, that we must contrive to leave this house without arousing suspicion. For the past week, Sarah and I have walked abroad together each day. Can we make use of that fact?"

"It will serve excellently!" he agreed eagerly. "Do

you know an inn called the Red Lion, at the end of the next street?"

"I have seen it. Are you lodged there?"

"No, at the shoemaker's nearby. He is a staunch Royalist and may be trusted absolutely. I will await you there."

"Charity, what of the servant who always accompanies us?" Sarah put in anxiously. "If we go out unattended it *will* arouse suspicion."

"Plague take the man, I had forgotten him!" Charity paused, frowning, but after a few moments her brow cleared again. "I have it, I think! When we reach the shoemaker's, Sarah, you must feign a sudden faintness, and I will take you within and ask that you may rest until you have recovered. Then after a little I will send the servant to fetch your sedan-chair to carry you home, and as soon as he has gone we may slip away." He glanced at Hal. "Is there another entrance to the house, so that no one will see us leave?"

"Yes, in an alley at the rear. I will have horses waiting nearby."

She nodded. "And when Taynton's servants return with the chair, the shoemaker may tell them that Sarah found herself recovered and that we left his house to start walking home. That may serve to divert suspicion from him."

"Yet a search is bound to be made!" Sarah sounded frightened. "If we are caught, we can look for no mercy from my husband or from Jonas."

Charity and Hal exchanged glances. They both knew that Sarah spoke truly, and both had a far clearer notion of what the penalty of failure would be; yet the

170

odds against the success of their plan were appalling. To ride out of Plymouth in broad daylight without being seen by someone who would remember them later if questioned by their pursuers was more than they dared to hope for. Some means of throwing those pursuers off the scent must be devised, and with that thought a gleam of mischief came into Charity's eyes.

"Mr Mordisford," she said abruptly, "would it be possible in so short a time to obtain a suit of men's clothes for me to wear?"

"Charity!" Sarah's tone was scandalised. "You would not do such a thing?"

"Why not? It is useless to pretend that my height is not unusual in a woman, for 'tis the one thing about me which is usually remembered, yet in a man it would be nothing out of the common. Moreover, those seeking us will be looking for two women, and therefore one woman and two men may well escape their attention."

"Upon my life, that is an excellent thought!" Hal agreed admiringly. "Nor does the obtaining of such disguise present any difficulty, for I have at my lodging the clothes I put off to assume the identity of John Sedgeworth. You and I are much of a height, Miss Charity, and they should fit you well enough for our purpose. My present attire is plain enough to pass for that of a serving-man, and Sarah can ride pillion behind me. Thus we should present an appearance so different from that which is likely to be described by our pursuers that no one will suspect us."

"It is to be hoped so," Charity replied dryly. "Now, sir, let us determine the hour at which we shall meet with you tomorrow, and then you must go. All these fine plans will come to naught if we arouse suspicion in this house now."

# 10

WHEN Charity awoke next morning the first thought which leapt to her mind was of the desperate venture planned for that day. Her heart beat fast with excitement, for though there were risks to be taken and dangers to be faced, it would mean an end at least to the weary waiting, the humble obedience to every unreasonable demand, the deference to beliefs and loyalties in direct and bitter conflict with her own. The prospect of freedom beckoned alluringly, and no matter what the cost, she felt at that moment that it could not be too dearly brought.

During the first part of the day, as throughout the previous evening, she watched Sarah anxiously for any hint of excitement or misgiving which might arouse suspicion, but to her relief none came. One thing only gave her cause for dismay, and that was the weather which that day was dull and overcast, with a blustering wind from the sea to set everything shaking and rattling, for if rain began to fall there would be no question of walking abroad. By noon, however, the clouds had begun to break, and though the wind remained as strong as ever, a few gleams of sunshine gave promise of a fine afternoon.

As the agreed time drew near the two young women made their usual preparations to go out. Sarah was by this time in a state of such trembling excitement that Charity was obliged to help her to dress, finding a warm wrap to put about her shoulders, and arrange her hair becomingly beneath the tall-crowned, feathered hat. She was tying her own black cloth hood beneath her chin when a serving-maid came to inform her that Captain Pennan had arrived to see her on a matter of urgent family business. Sarah and Charity exchanged a dismayed glance, and then the latter said as calmly as she could:

"Thank you! I will see him at once."

Sarah, waiting only until the maid had left them, clutched her cousin by the arm. "Charity, you cannot! All our plans will be overset."

"I must see him, love! He has come from Conyngton and may possibly bring word from Darrell. Wait for me here! At worst it can mean only a few minutes' delay."

Sarah seemed unconvinced but agreed because she had no choice, and Charity, hastening to the parlour, found Tom being entertained by Catherine and Mary. When they had greeted each other he turned to the two girls and said courteously:

"The message which I bring to Miss Shenfield from her aunt is of a most private nature. May I ask that you leave us alone while I tell her of it?"

Catherine looked resentful and a trifle suspicious, but since she could not with civility refuse the request, she went out of the room, taking her sister with her. Tom closed the door behind them and returned to Charity.

Taking her by the arm, he led her to the far side of the room, saying softly:

"Let us talk here! It would not surprise me if that sly little wench had her ear to the keyhole." He let go her arm and turned more fully to face her, and she saw that he looked exceedingly grave. "Miss Charity, it is my belief that great danger threatens Sir Darrell Conyngton."

Her heart seemed to stand still; she said with difficulty: "Tell me!"

"As you know," Tom replied quietly, "I shared your suspicion that Shenfield's insistence that you remain here served some purpose of his own, and his manner while I was at the Moat House did nothing to alter that opinion. Ellen and I have spied shamelessly upon him whenever opportunity offered, and today our vigilance was rewarded, for I overheard him talking to his mother. He told her that by tomorrow the weapon he had sought for would be in his hands, and Conyngton within his reach at last."

Charity stared at him, the colour draining from her face. "Was that all, sir? No indication of what the weapon might be?"

Tom shook his head. "No, none at all! Mrs Shenfield asked him what he meant, but he would reply only that it was better that she did not know. She accepted this without question, and said something about him having been right all the while and patience being the only sure way to his goal." He paused, looking at her with a troubled frown. "That is not all, Miss Charity! I heard something else, which convinced me beyond all doubt that the danger is real and pressing. Your aunt said, "What of Charity?" and Shenfield laughed and replied: "We shall be rid of her also, as I promised you. As soon as the other business is done, Stotewood may claim his bride, and I think we may depend upon him to break her spirit and bring her in time to a proper humility."

"Stotewood?" Charity repeated in a stupefied whisper. "Daniel Stotewood? Even Jonas would not dare!" She broke off as with a terrible clarity the implication of what Tom had said dawned upon her. "He would not dare," she repeated in a whisper, "as long as Darrell lives!"

Tom nodded. "Shenfield must be very sure of himself! I went straight to the Dower House, but Sir Darrell was not there and his servants could not or would not tell me where to find him. So I came to you instead."

"I am very grateful!" Charity spoke absently, her thoughts already racing ahead to what had best be done. She was afraid, for Darrell, for herself, for what this new danger might mean to Hal and Sarah, but anger against Jonas was stronger even than fear, and spurred her mind to work swiftly and clearly. Almost certainly, she thought, the weapon Jonas had spoken of was connected with the failure of the Royalist conspiracies, and therefore Hal might have some idea of what it could be; certainly he would know where Darrell could at present be found. With sudden decision she looked again at Tom.

"I *am* very grateful, Captain Pennan," she said quietly, "more grateful than I can ever tell. Your warning of this danger may perhaps afford us an opportunity to avoid it."

"You will need help to do so," he replied quietly.

"You know, I think, that you have only to tell me how."

She nodded. "I do know it, my friend, but it is not right that you should embroil yourself in this affair without knowing everything that is involved. I need no proof of your friendship towards *me*, but now I have to entrust you with secrets not my own, and whether you look upon what is intended as right or wrong, I must beg that you respect my confidence. Have I your word upon that?"

"Aye, with all my heart! You would not, I am convinced, lend yourself to anything dishonourable."

"As to that, sir, only God may judge," she replied with a sigh, and then, in a few brief sentences, described to him Hal's visit and the plans made for that day. Tom listened in silence, his thin, sun-bronzed face giving no clue to his thoughts.

"What Mrs Taynton does lies between God and her own conscience," he said when Charity had done, "though from what I know of the circumstances, I cannot find it in *my* heart to blame her. I take it that you wish me to meet you at the house of this shoe-maker?"

"If you will, sir, and you had best go at once, that you may be out of sight within before we come. It will not do for Mr Taynton's servant to see you there. Ask for John Sedgeworth, and bid them tell him you come from me with a message from Lady Linslade."

Tom agreed to this, and took his departure without more delay, while Charity returned to Sarah. She thought it better not to tell her cousin of the disturbing news Tom Pennan had brought until the first part of their escape had been accomplished, and, turning aside her anxious questions with a promise to answer them later, she summoned the manservant and they set off at a sober pace along the street.

All came to pass as they had planned. Their abrupt entry to the shoemaker's dark little shop was greeted with a fine show of astonishment and concern; the shoemaker's wife was summoned, and with many exclamations helped Sarah up the steep, twisting stair behind the shop; Charity paused to bid the servant wait below and then followed them.

In the room above, Hal Mordisford and Tom Pennan awaited them. Sarah gave a gasp of alarm when she saw Tom, but Hal came to take her hands in his, saying reassuringly:

"There is naught to fear, sweetheart! Captain Pennan is a friend." He looked at Charity. "This is ill news, Miss Charity!"

"Ill news, indeed!" she replied gravely. "Have you any suspicion, sir, what this weapon that Jonas prates of may be?"

He was frowning. "I can think of one thing only, but cannot see how Shenfield could know of it, much less hope to get it into his possession. There is a paper bearing the names of those concerned in the conspiracy of which Darrell is the leader, together with information regarding the forces each one could muster to fight for the King. It is the one piece of written evidence which exists, and if it fell into the hands of the authorities, it would be enough to hang every man named upon it."

"Where is this paper?" Charity asked sharply. "At the Dower House?"

Hal shook his head. "No, Sir Richard Linslade has it. It *was* in Darrell's possession, but one of Linslade's neighbours was growing faint-hearted and suspicious of his fellow-plotters, and Linslade besought Darrell to send him the paper to show to the man so that he might know all had set their hand to it and he need not fear betrayal."

"A fear well founded, it seems," Tom remarked bluntly, "if Shenfield has indeed got wind of this ill-advised document. When did Sir Darrell part with it?"

"He sent it to Dorringford by a trusted messenger three days since. Linslade is to bring it to their meeting today." Hal looked in dismay from Tom to Charity. "If Shenfield does know of that paper's existence, one thing is certain. There is a traitor among them!"

"Why in Heaven's name were they rash enough to set anything down in writing?" Charity beat her hands together in exasperation. "Darrell has said repeatedly that he would put his hand to no incriminating document."

"I believe he was unwillingly persuaded to it by his friends," Hal said bitterly. "It was to be a safeguard, they said. Where all were equally committed, one could not betray the rest without betraying himself."

Tom gave a short, angry laugh. "Find whence that ingenious suggestion came, and you will be in a fair way to finding your traitor. Who first spoke of it?"

"I know not! My service to the King has lain in travelling between the Court and His Majesty's supporters in England, and I have played little part in establishing our conspiracies here. I did not even know of this paper until Darrell told me of it the other day. Even then he was uneasy at letting it out of his possession." He was silent for a few moments, frowning in troubled thought, and then sighed and straightened his shoulders. "All this is to no avail! I must ride at once to the meeting-place to warn him."

Sarah, who had sunk down on a bench by the wall, had been listening in bewilderment and growing alarm to the swift exchange of talk, but if much of it was beyond her comprehension, those last words she understood only too well. A little sound of protest broke piteously from her lips, and she put out a hand to clutch at Hal's sleeve. He turned quickly to look at her, covering her hand with his own.

"My dear love, I have no choice! Men's lives are at stake!"

"No!" Charity spoke in a tone of firm resolution. "Sarah cannot return to Taynton's house, and your place, sir, is with her, just as mine is with Darrell. Tell me where he is to be found, and *I* will bear the warning."

"Miss Charity, you cannot! This is no task for a woman."

"You forget, my friend, that today I am to play a man's part. Is the disguise ready?"

"It is ready, but I will not let you attempt such a journey alone. The meeting-place is an inn more than five miles beyond Conyngton, and you do not even know the road. It is out of the question!"

"As to that, sir," Tom put in mildly, "I will gladly go with Miss Charity, or better still, carry the warning in her stead, if you will furnish me with some credential to prove to Sir Darrell that I come in good faith. I have met with him but once, when I bore Miss Charity's letter to the Dower House."

Hal's brow cleared a little, but Charity turned to look candidly at Tom. "This is an errand which may well end in prison, Captain Pennan," she said quietly. "We cannot ask you to take part in so perilous an undertaking."

"But you have not asked it of me," he pointed out. "I would prefer to bear the warning to Sir Darrell while you go with Mr Mordisford and your cousin, as you had planned, but if you insist upon going yourself—as I have no doubt you will—then nothing will prevent me from giving you my company on the journey, and such protection as I may."

For a few seconds Charity continued to regard him, and he looked steadily back at her with a hint of humour in his eyes. At length an answering gleam awoke in her own, and she said:

"Then I accept it, sir, with the deepest gratitude. You place me more deeply in your debt."

"There should be no talk of debts or gratitude between friends, Miss Charity," he replied lightly. "Now may I suggest that you make ready with no more delay, for the sooner we are all away from Plymouth, the better it will be."

II

In a dark, stuffy little room under the eaves, Sarah helped Charity to disguise herself. Since Hal was of slight build the suit of fine, dove-grey cloth fitted well enough to pass muster, and only the wide-topped, spurred boots of soft leather were uncomfortably large. When she was dressed, Charity unbound her hair and held out to Sarah the scissors she had brought with her. Sarah stared at her in dismay.

"Oh, Charity! Your beautiful hair!"

"It will grow again! Come, child, I cannot well perform the task myself."

She sat down on a wooden stool, and Sarah went reluctantly to work with comb and scissors, the heavy strands of black hair falling about her feet. When it was done, and Charity rose and turned to face her, she could not suppress an exclamation of surprise.

"Why, coz, you look so different! I would scarcely have believed it possible."

This was no more than the truth. In male attire Charity's height was no longer remarkable, and with her hair, released from the bondage of the severe cap, framing her face and falling on to her shoulders across the broad lace collar of the grey doublet, she looked far younger, a boy of sixteen or seventeen at most. She gave a little, half-rueful chuckle, and fingered one of her shortened tresses.

"I remember how, when I was a girl, I wished that I might wear my hair thus instead of being vexed with pins and ribbons. I never thought then that the wish would one day be granted."

She took Hal's sword and sword-belt from the peg where they hung and passed the baldrick over her head, settling it on her right shoulder. Then she picked up the cloak and the broad hat with its curling plume, and motioned to Sarah to precede her out of the room.

"We have done the best we can. Now let us see if my disguise will meet with the gentlemen's approval."

Hal was waiting for them in the room above the shop. Tom had already gone, leaving unobtrusively by the back door to avoid being seen by the waiting manservant, and Hal was alone with his troubled thoughts. The sound of the opening door roused him, and he turned to see Sarah coming into the room, followed by a slim, darkly handsome youth in whom, at first glance, he had some difficulty in recognising Charity Shenfield. She halted just within the room and regarded him questioningly.

"Well, sir? Will it suffice?"

"Excellently well, upon my word!" he said admiringly. "It is my belief that you might pass Jonas Shenfield himself in the street and not be recognised."

"Let us hope, however, that the disguise will not be put to that test," she replied dryly. "Where is Captain Pennan?"

"Gone ahead of us. We have appointed a convenient meeting-place outside the town. Now I will bid our host send Taynton's serving-man upon his fool's errand, and then we, too, may leave."

He went out, and Charity turned her attention to making some slight changes in Sarah's appearance. Hal had had the forethought to procure a voluminous cloak to cover her gown, and Charity herself had brought with her a mask such as ladies commonly wore when travelling to protect their complexions from the weather. With this in place, and Charity's black hood tied closely over her fair curls in place of her own hat, Sarah acquired an anonymity which her cousin hoped would be sufficient disguise.

They left the house, and went along the alley to a nearby courtyard where the shoemaker's son waited with horses. Charity was an excellent horsewoman, but she had not ridden astride since her madcap childhood, and she hoisted herself into the saddle hoping she was not betraying the misgivings she felt. The horse bearing

Hal and Sarah clattered out of the court and along the street, and Charity followed it closely. No one looked twice at so commonplace a sight as a lady riding pillion behind her serving-man, with a young gentleman as her escort, and since while they traversed the busy streets they were obliged to move at walking pace, Charity had time to accustom herself to the unfamiliar saddle and her even more unfamiliar attire.

Once free of the town they quickened their pace a little, and before long came up with Captain Pennan at the prearranged spot. He greeted them cheerfully, looking at Charity with mingled surprise and admiration.

"You make a gallant youth, Miss Charity," he told her with a grin, "and wear your sword as to the manner born."

"That is easy enough to do, sir, as long as I am not called upon to use it," she setorted, "and while I do wear this guise I think you had best call me Charles. 'Tis a good Royalist name, and not too unlike my own."

For the next few miles their roads lay together, but at length they reached the cross-roads where they must part to reach their different destinations. There was no time for prolonged farewells. Charity leaned across to bestow a swift kiss upon Sarah, and then held out her hand to Hal.

"Watch well over her, my friend," she said with a fleeting smile, "and good fortune go with you."

"And with you, Miss Charity," he replied gravely. "God grant we see you and Darrell with us before we embark for France."

"Amen to that," she replied seriously, "but if the

weather favours your crossing, do not stay for us. Whatever befalls, there is no more that you can do here."

He made no reply to this beyond a firm handclasp, and then with a word of farewell to Tom he urged his horse forward again. Charity watched them for a moment and then looked at her companion.

"Let us go on," she said in a low voice, "and I pray God we do not come too late."

He nodded, and they spurred their horses on again, making the best speed they could. The sky was clearer now, but the afternoon was waning and in the pale, spring sunlight the shadows had already begun to lengthen. The boisterous wind buffeted the riders, plucking at their cloaks and rippling the plumes in their hats, and only when the narrow road ran between steep banks did they find shelter from it. As they drew near to Conyngton St John, Tom reined his horse closer to Charity's and said briefly:

"Do we ride through the village?"

She frowned. "We have no choice! The river will be running full and deep at this time of year, and to reach the nearest ford we would need to go miles out of our way. You will be recognised, of course, but any who see you will suppose you to be on your way to the Moat House, and it is to be hoped that no one will recognise me."

"It is to be hoped indeed," he agreed with a laugh. "Forward, then, friend Charles!"

In spite of her bold words Charity knew it was in Conyngton St John that the greatest danger of discovery would lie. The villagers would not betray her to Jonas, but Dr Malperne, if they encountered him, would be quick to do so, and might succeed in preventing her from reaching Darrell. That was her foremost thought, her greatest fear; not for herself, in spite of what was intended towards her, but for him. In this sudden, deadly danger one idea, one desire wholly possessed her mind, and she was conscious only of the need to reach him, to be at his side whatever befell.

They came in sight of the village, and Charity pulled her broad-brimmed hat lower on her brow and looked neither to right nor left at they clattered across the bridge and along the curving street. She was acutely aware of the familiarity of her surroundings. The inn and the water-mill; the forge where the smith's fire glowed and his hammer rang; the village green with its stocks and whipping-post; the church tower rising among the yew-trees. She did not need to look at any of these things to be aware of them. This was her home, and Darrell's, and even if the present danger could be averted, it might be years before either of them dwelt here again.

After what seemed an eternity they were safely beyond the village, and the horses' speed slackened as they began to climb the long hill, on the crest of which the desolate ruins of Conyngton were outlined against the evening sky. Then the manor was behind them, they had forded the rushing stream in the next valley and were crossing Jonas Shenfield's land. As they passed the entrance to the track which led to the Moat House, Charity glanced anxiously along it but could detect no sign of life.

Nevertheless, the sense of her kinsman's presence and the authority he wielded here oppressed her, and she was thankful when at last the Shenfield lands had been left behind them. They were nearing their goal now, the lonely inn of which Hal Mordisford had told them. Their road had brought them northward and eastward from Conyngton St John, sweeping in a great curve to skirt part of the forbidding waste of Dartmoor, which reared its barren slopes and granite ramparts a short way off, wild and eerie in the fading light.

They found the inn at last, a squat stone building standing where four ways met on the very edge of the Moor. Only the faded signboard creaking in the wind showed that this was indeed an inn, for the door was shut fast and the windows closely shuttered, with only a feeble gleam of light showing here and there through cracks in the stout wood. In this bleak place the wind was fiercer than it had been in the sheltered valleys, and the shrieking of it masked the sound of their approach. They halted beneath the swinging sign and for a moment or two sat looking at the unwelcoming face of the house. Then Charity slid stiffly from the saddle, and Tom, dismounting also, tethered the horses to an iron ring hanging from the wall beside the door.

So dark and inhospitable did the place appear that it was almost surprising when the door swung open at a touch, revealing a narrow, stone-flagged passage dimly lit by a rush-light in an iron holder on the wall. The place appeared to be deserted, and yet at the first sound of their footsteps on the stone floor a man materialised out of the shadows at the far end of the passage, a stocky, grey-haired countryman who eyed them suspiciously. Tom's cheery greeting met with a guarded response, but undeterred by this he went on briskly:

"We are seeking Sir Darrell Conyngton. Will you

tell him that Tom Pennan desires to speak with him?"

The man stared stolidly back at him. "What makes 'ee think Sir Darrell be here?"

"We know that he came here to meet certain friends," Tom replied pleasantly, "and as we have just ridden from Conyngton St John without encountering him, it seems likely that he tarries here yet. I pray you, make haste! Our business brooks no delay!"

The inn-keeper shook his head. "Sir Darrell and the other gentlemen be at supper, and they said naught to me of expecting other guests. If 'ee seeks food and drink 'ee can have it, otherwise ye'd best begone."

"Now look you, my friend," Tom began impatiently, but Charity, who had hitherto remained in the background, touched his arm to silence him. She stepped past him and, pulling off her glove, slid from her finger the ring which Darrell had given her the previous summer. Holding it out to the inn-keeper, she said quietly:

"I pray you, show that to Sir Darrell! If he will not see us then, I give you my word that we will go."

The man looked doubtful, but he took the ring and, with another suspicious look from one to the other, went back the way he had come, Charity stood staring after him, and after a minute or so Tom, who had been narrowly regarding her, said carelessly:

"I'll warrant yon surly dog of an inn-keeper will give no thought to our horses! I'd best go myself to see them stabled."

She nodded, casting him a grateful glance, and he went out, the light flickering wildly in the draught as the door opened and closed. Charity drew back to pace into the shadows, for a familiar footstep was approaching and a moment later Darrell emerged from the darkness which obscured the other end of the passage. Seeing only a slight, boyish figure waiting there, he halted in sudden suspicion, saying imperiously:

"What trickery is this? I was told that Captain Pennan was here!" Receiving no immediate reply, he clapped a hand to his sword, adding more sharply still: "Who are you?"

Charity drew a deep breath. "One to whom *your* safety, Darrell, is the most precious thing in the world," she replied unsteadily, and stepped forward so that the light fell directly upon her face.

### III

There was an instant of utter silence, and then Darrell said in a stunned tone: "Charity! In God's name, what brings you here, and in *that* guise?"

She looked steadily back at him, heightened colour in her cheeks but a challenge in her dark eyes. "Does it matter, Darrell, in what guise I come? I would not care if you came to me in the rags of a beggar."

"Oh, my love!" With two swift strides he had reached her and caught her in his arms, crushing her lips beneath his own, and for a few rapturous moments the terror and the heartbreak could be forgotten. Then Darrell said incredulously: "Little one, you did not come alone all the way from Plymouth?"

"No, Captain Pennan rode with me. He is looking to our horses." She looked gravely up at him. "He is a true friend to us, Darrell! Were it not for him we should have had no warning of the danger which now threatens you."

As briefly as she could, she told him what Tom had

189

learned at the Moat House, and of Hal's suspicion of the form the danger might take, though for the present she kept to herself the plans which Jonas had made for her. She had barely finished when Tom returned, and Darrell, holding out his hands to him, said frankly:

"I am deeply indebted to you, Captain Pennan, not merely for your warning, but also for bringing Miss Shenfield safely to me."

"It will be time enough to speak of thanks, Sir Darrell, when the danger has been averted," Tom replied bluntly, though he grasped the proffered hand readily enough. "If Mr Mordisford is right, there is some ugly treachery afoot."

"So it would seem, sir, and the sooner the truth is discovered, the better," Darrell agreed, and looked again at Charity. "Would you obey me, my dear, if I bade you have food and rest here, and then let Captain Pennan take you back to the Dower House?"

She shook her head. "No, Darrell, I would not! Whatever is discovered tonight, and whatever is decided upon, I am determined not to be parted from you again."

"Obstinate jade!" he said softly. "I would I might insist upon it, but there is no time now to waste in arguments which I well know would be fruitless. Come, then!" He turned to Tom. "Your most prudent course, sir, would be to return with all speed to Plymouth or to the Moat House."

"No doubt, Sir Darrell, but prudence was never among my virtues," Tom retorted with a grin. "I, too, will see the business through to the end."

Darrell made a gesture of resignation, and beckoned them to follow him along the passage. So they came to a small, low-pitched room where a fire burned cheerily on a wide hearth, and half a dozen men were grouped about a table which still bore the remains of a meal. They looked up in surprise and some dismay as Darrell led his companions into the room, and one of them, a thin, anxious-looking man in black, said sharply:

"Sir Darrell, who are these gentlemen?"

"They are friends for whose loyalty and discretion I can vouch," Darrell replied briefly. "They come, gentlemen, to bring us a warning."

Charity, pausing just inside the room where the full light of the candles did not reach, recognised Sir Richard Linslade in the group about the table, and another vaguely familiar face which she identified after a moment as that of Japhet Chawton, the man who had come upon her and Darrell one summer morning in the gardens at Conyngton. The others were unknown to her, and though most of them seemed ready to accept Darrell's brief introduction, it appeared that the gentleman in black was less easily satisfied.

"If they are friends, sir," he said querulously, "let us know their names."

"My name, sir, is Thomas Pennan," Tom informed him equably, "and I am a sea-captain from Plymouth. I counsel you to listen at once to what Sir Darrell has to tell you. Believe me, it is news of far greater urgency than the names of those who bring it."

The thin man acknowledged this with a curt nod, but his gaze went past Tom to the slim figure by the door. Richard Linslade, who had been looking very hard in the same direction, spoke to forestall him.

"Let be, Anstead, in God's name, and let us hear what this warning may be."

Mr Anstead looked from one to the other, his suspicions sharpened rather than soothed by this intervention. "You all seem vastly anxious to keep secret the young gentleman's identity," he complained. "By your leave, gentlemen, I must insist upon knowing it."

"So be it!" Darrell spoke curtly, an undertone of anger in his voice, and turned to lead Charity forward. "Since Mr Anstead gives me no choice, I must tell you that this is Miss Shenfield, who has come here at no small risk to herself to warn us of possible betrayal." He paused, looking haughtily from one astonished face to another with a distinct challenge in his eye. "Miss Shenfield, gentlemen, is my future wife."

"Shenfield?" Mr Anstead repeated in a voice charged with suspicion. "That is a name which sounds uneasily in company such as ours."

"God's light! Will you be bickering over trifles until all is lost?" Darrell brought his hand down on the table with a force which made the dishes rattle. "I spoke of betrayal, Anstead, of a possible traitor among us! Is that of less importance than the names of the good friends who bring us warning of it?" He did not wait for a reply, but turned instead to Sir Richard. "Linslade, where is the paper I sent you?"

"Safe, as I told you!" Sir Richard bent down and drew a folded paper from a hiding-place in his boot. "It has not left my possession since I received it, and no one has seen it save Anstead, to reassure whom you sent it to me."

Slowly Darrell reached out and took the paper, looking at it with a faint, puzzled frown, and Charity, staring at it also, was not certain whether her own feeling was of relief or dismay. The fatally incriminating document was safe, yet Jonas was confident of his power to destroy Darrell, and if this were not the weapon he meant to use, where did the danger lie?

She glanced at Tom and saw that his perplexity equalled her own. Then Darrell, who had unfolded the paper to scan its contents, rapped out an oath and bent closer to the candles, studying the document intently while they all stared at him with returning uneasiness. At last he raised his head and looked slowly around the circle of anxious faces, his own pale and very stern.

"There is treachery here indeed, my friends," he said quietly. "This document is forged."

A profound silence greeted his words, a silence charged with shock, dismay and disbelief. The wind moaned round the house and rattled the stout shutters, and within the room, men looked suddenly upon the face of death. At last one of them said in a low voice:

"God help us! Conyngton, are you certain?"

"Quite certain!" Darrell laid the paper on the table and stood looking down at it. " 'Tis skillfully done, I own, and might well have served its purpose had I been given no cause to study it closely, but it is a forgery none the less. Yet it was not so, I swear, when I parted with it."

In the pause which followed, Tom moved very quickly to the door and set his back against it. Sir Richard rose slowly to his feet, looking around the table at the faces now turned towards him in doubt, inquiry and even faint suspicion. In his own face there showed both anger and dismay.

"Is this to accuse *me* of treachery, Conyngton? God defend me! Have I not as much to lose as any of you?"

Mr Anstead said accusingly: "Your wife is sister to Jonas Shenfield!"

"And Conyngton's promised bride is his cousin, and Captain Pennan his brother-in-law!" Linslade retorted with furious mockery. "On those grounds you might just as well accuse Sir Darrell himself of betraying us!"

"Wait!" Darrell spoke in a tone of firm command to check the brewing quarrel. "Nothing is to be gained by flinging wild accusations one against the other. Only three people could have substituted this forgery for the original. Myself, who kept the paper; Sir Richard, who has had it in his possession for the past three days; or he who bore it from Conyngton to Dorringford." His stern glance came to rest on the plump, inconspicuous man who sat so quietly at the foot of the table. "You, Japhet Chawton!"

There was another pause while his companions considered this. Charity, seated in Darrell's chair at the head of the table, while he stood beside her, realised that what he had said was true, and yet to her the identity of the traitor seemed unimportant compared to the horrifying fact that the original document, with its power to destroy them all, must even now be in Jonas's hands. Then through the daze of horror which possessed her she heard Linslade say sharply:

"*Three* days, did you say? That paper came into my hands but yesterday! Anstead, you were with me! You can bear out what I say."

"Aye, that's true!" Mr Anstead agreed slowly. "And I was with you because you expected to have received it sooner." He broke off abruptly, as though another thought had just occurred to him, and then thrust back his stool and rose to his feet, pointing an accusing hand at Japhet Chawton. "My God! It was you who first sowed the seeds of doubt in my mind, and suggested that I demand to see the paper again to assure myself that the others had as much at stake as I."

"And if I mistake not," Darrell added sternly, "it was Chawton who first suggested that such a document should be drawn up. So now we have the truth, gentlemen! We have been trepanned, tricked by a decoy duck in Jonas Shenfield's pay into furnishing evidence against ourselves."

Charity, looking along the length of the table at Chawton, saw a flicker of fear cross the man's round, pink face, and his eyes glance furtively towards the door as though contemplating escape, but Tom still leaned there, blocking the only way out of the room. Then Darrell left her side and strode round the table to Chawton and gripped him by the front of his doublet, jerking him to his feet.

"That is the truth, is it not?" he said savagely. "Shenfield bribed you to trick and betray us?"

Japhet Chawton, held thus ignominiously prisoner, aware of the other men rising to their feet and crowding around him, realised that there was no hope of denial or escape, and instead fell back upon bluster. Staring up into the set face of his captor, he said mockingly:

"A truth, Sir Darrell, which you have discovered too late. The real Japhet Chawton has lain prisoner these twelve months past in Taunton gaol, and Mr Shenfield has paid me well to unmask your damnable conspiracies. If you kill me, it will be but an added count against you when you stand your trial, and will profit you not at all. By this time the evidence is in the hands of the authorities."

Darrell released him, and he dropped back on to the bench, smoothing his rumpled garments, while a babble of talk broke out among the other men as argument, accusation and conflicting advice were bandied to and fro. Darrell said nothing. He turned and looked at Charity, and as their glances met, each read in the other's eyes the knowledge that this was the end, that even the hope of a future together no longer existed. He moved towards her, and she rose and came to meet him, putting her hands into his and looking up into his face. The angry, frightened, desperate men clustered about the table were forgotten, and it was as though they were alone in the dark little room.

It was Tom's voice which finally recalled them to awareness of their surroundings. The voices of the other men had risen to an angry clamour, but Tom was accustomed to making himself heard above the roaring of Atlantic storms, and his first words smote them all into silence.

"It may be that all is not yet lost!" Having thus captured their attention, he left his place by the door and advanced to the table, his keen glance flickering over them all and finally coming to rest on Darrell. "This morning I heard Jonas Shenfield say that he expected the evidence to be in his hands *by tomorrow*. Now it seems to me that in a place where Shenfield is so bitterly hated, and Sir Darrell's family so much beloved, this treacherous dog would find it difficult to meet with his master without Sir Darrell learning of it. Therefore, unless he carries the original document with him now—

which we may easily discover—he must have concealed it in some prearranged hiding place."

"By God, sir, you may be right!" Darrell exclaimed. "Shenfield is too careful of his own safety to risk meeting his hired Judas anywhere in Conyngton St John."

"That may be so," Mr Anstead struck in irritably, "but you say Chawton had the paper from you three days ago."

"And Linslade received the forgery from him yesterday! To make so exact a copy must have taken a considerable time, and Chawton could not have lingered in Conyngton St John to carry out so delicate a task. It is my belief that the original was still in his possession when he came to Dorringford." Darrell swung abruptly to face Chawton. "Well, fellow? If you value your life, you will be frank with us!"

Japhet Chawton looked up at him, his cunning, cherubic face wrinkled with mockery. "You are shrewd, Sir Darrell, you and the Captain yonder, and have the matter very nearly correct, but it can avail you nothing. The evidence was concealed during last night, and Mr Shenfield will have it in his possession by now."

"I think not!" Tom put in quietly. "When Shenfield rode out this morning with his servant, Stotewood, I heard him tell his mother that he had business at a village near Kingsbridge and would not reach home again until evening. It is just possible that we might recover that evidence first."

Chawton shook his head. "You might, sir, if you knew where to look for it, but you do not. Nor do I intend to tell you."

For a second or two Tom considered him in silence. Then he set his foot on the bench beside Chawton, and with his elbow on his knee leaned towards the other man in a manner almost confidential.

"As you know, my friend, I am a seafarer," he said amiably, "and in the course of my travels I have learned any number of ingenious devices for loosening stubborn tongues. Would you like to know how the Carib Indians deal with their captured enemies, or the Inquisitors of Spain torment men's bodies for the good of their souls? Or shall I teach you how the sea-rovers of the Caribbean persuade their prisoners to divulge the whereabouts of hidden valuables? There are many cunning tricks I could perform upon your body, and I am sure that these gentlemen you have betrayed would find them diverting."

Chawton passed his tongue across dry lips, for this was a turn of events he had not foreseen. "You would not dare!" he said with an attempt at boldness. "This is England, Captain, and not some pirate ship or barbarous, God-forgotten island."

"Would I not?" Tom retorted pleasantly. "Bethink you, Mr Chawton, that the lives of seven men hang in the balance, to say nothing of Miss Shenfield's safety, and my own, and then ask yourself again whether or not I would dare."

Darrell moved forward so that he, too, stood close to Chawton. "Let me remind you," he said grimly, "that this house is as isolated as any ship upon the high seas, and every soul within it united against you. We may do here as we will, and afterwards . . ." He shrugged. "The Moor keeps many secrets. It will keep ours as safely."

Japhet Chawton looked from him to Tom, and thence to the implacable, desperate faces of the other men, and the sweat of fear started on his brow. Last of all he looked at Charity.

"Madam," he said hoarsely, "help me! You at least will not stand aside and let them torture me. No woman would!"

Charity stepped forward until she stood once more beside Darrell, looking down into Chawton's face, which was livid now with the pallor of terror. Her own face was pale, the lips set, the dark eyes filled with contempt and anger.

"You are mistaken, Mr Chawton," she said coldly. "Has no one ever told you that in defence of that which she loves, a woman can be more ruthless than any man?" She turned to Darrell. "Is there some other room where I may wait while you do what has to be done?"

He nodded, taking her arm to lead her to the door, and the other men moved aside to let them pass. Chawton watched her departure with horror-stricken, disbelieving eyes, and then, as Tom's hand fell heavily upon his shoulder, turned his head to stare in terror into the Captain's grimly smiling face.

# 11

OUTSIDE in the passage Charity turned anxiously to Darrell. "You do not really intend . . ." She left the sentence unfinished, and nodded towards the door of the room they had just left.

"We shall do what we must," he replied in a low voice. "It may be that the threat alone will suffice. I hope it will!"

He would say no more, but led her to the kitchen where the inn-keeper and his wife and two young sons were gathered about the fire. Darrell exchanged a few softly spoken words with the man, and a place was made for Charity on the big wooden settle by the hearth. She sat down, conscious now of weariness but indifferent to it as her anxious thoughts circled endlessly around the disaster which had overtaken Darrell and his friends.

The minutes dragged slowly by. The woman of the house brought her a wooden bowl full of hot soup, and some coarse bread, and she ate it reluctantly, not wishing to offend. The two boys chattered together in low voices, with occasional bursts of the inconsequential laughter of childhood, and the wind, which seemed to have increased to the force of a gale, howled round the house and thudded like distant gunfire in the wide chimney. Once Charity started violently, thinking she had heard a cry from the room she had left, but the walls of the inn were thick and in the clamour of the wind she could not be certain.

At last, when in spite of her nagging fears the warmth of the fire was beginning to make her feel drowsy, the door opened again and Darrell beckoned to her. She got up hastily and followed him into the passage, casting an apprehensive glance towards the other room, but the door was shut and only an indistinguishable murmur of voices came from behind it.

"We have learned what we needed to know," Darrell said shortly, and from his voice, and what she could see of his face in the feeble glow of the rushlight, she could tell that he was in the grip of a consuming anger. "The paper is hidden at Conyngton, in the ruins of the house. Jonas has had the infernal impudence to use my own home as a means of communicating with his hired decoy."

She started at him, wondering why neither of them had guessed it. The ruined manor, so lonely, yet so easily accessible from either the village or the Moat House, was the perfect place for private meetings, as she and Darrell had learned; why not also the hiding-place for messages from Chawton to his master? Jonas must have derived enormous satisfaction from the arrangement. It was the sort of petty triumph that delighted him.

"That day last summer when we saw Chawton at the manor," she said suddenly. "Was it that which brought him there?"

"Very likely!" Darrell's tone was curt. "Charity, I ride now to Conyngton to learn if the paper still lies hidden there. If it does, I shall destroy it. If not . . ." He did not complete the sentence, but instead set his hands on her shoulders, looking down into her face with a sudden softening of his own. "Little one, I want you to go back to the Dower House. Linslade and Pennan will go with you. If I come not by morning, take the jewels—you know where they are hidden—and let Tom Pennan take you to join Hal and Sarah. Go with them to France. Thus, at least, you will be free of Jonas."

She heard him out to the end, her gaze fixed gravely on his face, and then shook her head. "No, Darrell," she said quickly. "I told you a while since that I would not be parted from you again. I will come with you to Conyngton."

"Love, you cannot! I mean to take the track across the Moor—it will save at least two miles."

"When have I ever shrunk from riding on the Moor?" she challenged him with a faint smile. "Tonight its most fearsome legends holds no terrors for me, for I fear one thing only—that you and I may be parted, not to meet again. So take me with you! I swear you will not need to curb your pace on my account."

He sighed, looking at her with a faint, rueful smile. "If only there were time to dissuade you, or to find some means of compelling you to obey me, but every moment is precious. Come, then, my heart! If naught else will content you, we will ride together."

He led her out of the inn by another door, and so to the stable where the inn-keeper summoned from the kitchen by Sir Richard, was already saddling Darrell's horse, and Linslade himself and Tom Pennan stood talking in low tones. When they learned that Charity meant to accompany Darrell, Sir Richard started to protest, but Tom interrupted him without ceremony.

"You waste breath, Sir Richard! If Sir Darrell cannot dissuade her, be sure that we cannot. She will need a fresh horse, though! Ours are still weary from the journey from Plymouth."

"Then she had best take mine," Linslade said resignedly, "though to my mind this is a folly which should not be permitted. Better by far that she should return with us to the Dower House."

He turned away to see the saddling of the horse, and Tom looked at Charity with a wry grin. "He speaks truth," he remarked, "and having said that I will say no more. We shall meet presently at the Dower House, and God grant it be a merry meeting, with all danger past!"

The horses were led out of the stable and the two riders mounted. Darkness had long since fallen, but a waning moon peered fitfully between ragged, wind-torn clouds, dimly revealing the shuttered house, the lonely cross-roads and the grim outline of the Moor against the luminous sky. A brief word of farewell was spoken, and the horses moved away, their pace quickening as they started along the track which wound upwards to the Moor. The innkeeper shook his head, and furtively made a sign to ward off evil.

"God shield 'em," he muttered. "There be more dangers yonder than men know of!"

His words expressed the general opinion of his time, for superstition peopled the desolate expanse of Dartmoor with witches and demons, and few men would have ventured into it after dark, even for the most pressing reasons. The track which Darrell and Charity followed, however, crossed only the fringe of the wilderness, and though they had both been born and reared almost within sight of the dreaded Moor, and had absorbed its weird legends in their nurseries, tonight the earthly danger which threatened them outweighed any dread of the powers of darkness.

Yet it was an eerie journey. The gale shrieked across the waste of bog and heather and around the granite tors as though it were the baying of the fabled Yeth Hounds, while the racing cloud shadows might have been demon hunters urging on the hellish pack. The two riders were mere specks in the vast, savage landscape, dwarfed to nothingness by the immensity of the Moor. The wind buffeted them without mercy, tearing at their cloaks, stopping the very breath in their throats. Charity's hat was plucked from her head and whirred away into the darkness and her hair whipped across her face in stinging strands. She rode with bent head, dazed by the fury of the gale, conscious only of the need to control the spirited horse she bestrode, and to keep pace with Darrell's dimseen figure moving a yard or two ahead of her.

At last the wildness of the Moor was behind them and they were descending into the gentler countryside around Conyngton, and finally, in a narrow lane which ran between high banks barely a quarter of a mile from the manor, Darrell drew rein and turned to his companion.

"We will cross the park from the end of the lane, and leave our horses in that clump of oak trees just out of sight of the gatehouse," he said softly. "Better to go forward on foot and give no warning of our approach." He leaned forward, peering at her in the dim moonlight. "How is it with you, sweetheart?"

"I am well enough!" She forced a weary smile, pushing the tangled hair back from her face. "Have no fear, Darrell! I will not falter now, within reach of our goal."

"Do I not know it?" He reached out to clasp her hand for a moment in a hard, reassuring grip. "My valiant love!"

The horses moved forward again, and so, a few minutes later, they came to the clump of oak trees and passed into its shadow. Darrell tethered their mounts to a low-hanging branch and then, with Charity's hand in his, led the way across the rough grass towards the dark bulk of the gatehouse. Just as they reached it a thick cloud veiled the moon, but as they paused in the blackness beneath the broad arch, Charity clutched at Darrell's arm.

"Look yonder!"

They stood staring across the forecourt to where a feeble glimmer of light moved erratically in the gaunt cavern of the shattered Hall. Darrell said under his breath: "Jonas! Then there may yet be time. Little one, bide here!"

He thrust her gently into the gate-keeper's room, and then he had gone from her into the darkness. She waited for a moment, listening intently, but could hear nothing save the blustering wind, the rustle of young leaves, the creak of straining boughs. She stepped out from the doorway and moved softly in the direction of the terrace.

As she reached the foot of the steps she heard Darrell stumble over some obstacle as he entered the ruined house, heard the rattle of stone and his involuntary, hastily stifled curse. Immediately the gleam of light within the ruins was quenched, and she felt her way up the steps and across the terrace in utter blackness. Then as she reached the house the veil of cloud lifted, and the pale face of the moon peered down once more into the roofless Hall.

From the shadows of what had once been the main entrance Charity saw, framed in the broken doorway, the two men confronting each other, Darrell halfway across the Hall, Jonas standing close to the gaping mouth of the great fireplace. A dark lantern stood on the flagstones at his feet and in one hand he held a levelled pistol. Darrell's sword was in his hand, the moonlight glinting dully on the slender blade, but Jonas laughed and shook his head.

"No, Conyngton," he said with a sneer, "I shall not cross swords with you again, now or ever. It is my ambition to see you hang, but if you make any move against me now I will pistol you where you stand. The document I carry here"—he laid his free hand on his breast—"is sufficient warrant for your death."

Charity stole forward until she crouched behind a pile of fallen stone just within the Hall, racking her brain for some means of aiding Darrell, of diverting Jonas's attention long enough for the other man to overpower him. She heard Darrell make some reply, but his words were lost in the voice of the wind and the demented creaking of a branch somewhere above her. Jonas shrugged, and laughed again, savouring to the full this moment of triumph when all that he most ardently desired was within his reach at last.

She bit her lip in agonised despair, her gaze frantically raking the ruined Hall in search of inspiration which did not come. With another fierce gust of wind the creak of tortured wood sounded more clearly than before, a little cloud of dust whirled about her and a tiny fragment of falling stone stung her cheek. The trifling pain roused her mind to an awareness of what this meant, to the fact that no tree could grow there, so high up amid the decaying walls, and with sudden urgency she stared up and around, trying to trace the source of the sound.

At last, guided by another rattle of falling stone, she found it, outlined against the sky. A huge, charred beam, one of those which had supported the lofty roof of the Hall and which now jutted starkly from the blackened wall close to the crumbling pinnacle of the great chimney. She looked, and blinked, and looked again, for it seemed that the vast baulk of timber was moving, swaying like the branch she had at first imagined it to be. For perhaps five seconds she stared at it, thinking that this was some trick of the fitful moonlight and the hurrying clouds, and then, with an awful awareness of the truth, sprang from her hiding-place with a scream of warning and darted towards Darrell.

There came the flash and sharp report of Jonas's pistol, and then a rumbling roar as the whole world was filled with hurtling stone and whirling clouds of dust that blotted out the moonlight. Darrell seized her and flung her to the ground, shielding her with his own body, and she clung tightly to him, convinced that they were both to die here in the crashing ruins of Conyngton. Then gradually the noise lessened and died away, and she opened her eyes and looked beyond Darrell's shoulder to see the dust settling in eddying wind-tossed clouds that moved like ghosts in the pale moonlight.

Darrell hoisted himself to his knees, dust and fragments of stone showering from his clothes as he moved. Charity struggled into a sitting position and looked about her, seeing the broken outline of the walls strangely altered now where the great chimney had crashed down, and that part of the Hall where Jonas had stood blocked by a mountain of fallen masonry. Darrell helped her up and they stood clinging to each other, bruised and shaken and choked with dust, scarcely able to believe that they had escaped without serious hurt. Then Darrell said hoarsely:

"Jonas!"

He stumbled away from her towards the huge pile of stone, and she followed him very slowly, for her limbs seemed to be made of lead and every step demanded enormous effort. She saw Darrell stoop and pick up some small object from among the scattered stone and rubble, and the dull gleam of metal showed her that it was the pistol. He went forward again, and then halted with a stifled exclamation, flinging out his hand to keep her back, and though she stopped obediently she could not avoid seeing the huddled figure almost buried by the tumbled stone. One arm was outstretched as though in a last, frantic effort to escape, and the broken flagstones beneath were darkly stained. After a long moment, Darrell said in a low voice:

"Go into the garden, Charity, and wait for me there. I will do what I can."

Too weary and shaken to protest, she turned away

and went with dragging steps towards the entrance. A few yards away she stumbled over Darrell's sword, and as though in a dream picked it up and went on with it in her hand. When she reached the terrace she sank down on the topmost step, laid the sword carefully beside her and bowed her head on her hands while tears of shock and exhaustion trickled unheeded down her cheeks. How long she sat there she did not know, but at last Darrell's footsteps roused her and she looked up to see him beside her, tall and grave-faced in the moonlight. He held a folded paper which was patched with dark stains.

"Jonas is dead," he said in a low voice. "I think he died instantly. There is no more that we can do."

He stopped and picked up his sword and sheathed it again, and then took Charity by the arm and helped her to her feet. She leaned wearily against him, lifting towards him a white face streaked with dirt and tears and framed by tangled hair. Darrell raised his hand and gently touched her wet cheek.

"There is no more that we can do," he said again. "Let us go home."

II

A cuckoo was calling not far off, and its sweet, monotonous voice was the first thing to reach Charity's waking senses. She opened her eyes to see daylight peeping through the drawn curtains of the bed, and lay for a little while staring at it and wondering why she was waking in unfamiliar surroundings. Then slowly recollection of the previous day stirred in her mind, and she realised that she was at the Dower House.

Dimly, as though it were a dream already half forgotten, she remembered the return from Conyngton, and how, utterly exhausted, she had almost fallen from the saddle into Darrell's arms. She remembered being carried within, a glimpse of the anxious faces of Tom Pennan and Richard Linslade, then of the women servants who had undressed her and washed her face and combed the tangles from her hair. After that she had slept, deeply and dreamlessly, which was strange after such hectic adventures, so many torturing fears.

She reached out and drew aside the curtain, blinking in the brightness of the sunlight which spilled into the room. The day must be well advanced, she thought, and sat up, aware of bruises, and of stiff and aching limbs which were a legacy of the long, unaccustomed hours in the saddle. The clothes she had worn the day before lay, brushed and neatly folded, on a stool nearby, and since she had no others she put them on. There was a mirror in the room, so that for the first time she was able to see herself in her borrowed attire, and was surprised and not ill-pleased by the comely youth who looked back at her from the glass.

When she went downstairs she found Sir Richard with Darrell, but after exchanging greetings with her he made some excuse to leave them. Darrell held out his hands to her with a smile and she went gladly into his arms. For the first time her kinsman's threatening shadow did not lie across their happiness, and though there were still difficulties awaiting them the one insuperable barrier had been cast down.

"Darrell, what will follow now?" she asked anxiously.

"Has Jonas's death yet been discovered?"

He shook his head. "Not yet, I believe! We had word from the village this morning that he had disappeared, but no one then knew whence. The story goes that he left the Moat House on foot last night after they had supped, and did not return. His servants have been searching for him since dawn, and that is how news of his disappearance became known in the village. We can do naught but wait. It will not do to betray any knowledge of what has befallen him."

"No, of course not!" Frowning, she moved to a day-bed which stood near the window, and sat down. "There will be messengers from Plymouth, too, arriving at the Moat House this day." She looked up questioningly. "What has become of Captain Pennan?"

"He returned to the Moat House as soon as news came that Jonas could not be found, and will bring us word of what befalls." Darrell came to sit beside her, taking her hands in his. "Little one, why did you not tell me of the infamous thing Jonas intended towards you?"

She shrugged. "It would have angered you to no purpose, and all that mattered to me then was to avert the danger which threatened you. Darrell, it has been averted? You have destroyed that paper?"

"Both it and its false counterpart, as soon as we returned last night. I have sent to tell the others that all is well, and John Parrish is bearing the good news to Hal and Sarah."

"What of the man Chawton? Suppose he should lay information against you?"

There was a long pause, and then Darrell said with a frown: "That will not happen, I give you my word, but I wish you to know no more than that."

She looked sharply at him, but something in his face prevented her from probing deeper. Japhet Chawton, hired spy and traitor, was more despicable even than Jonas, who had been driven by an overmastering hatred; if he had met with a fate similar to that of his master it was no more than just, and she could feel no pity for him.

It was past noon when Captain Pennan returned, and Darrell, Charity and Sir Richard were at dinner. In answer to their anxiously inquiring looks Tom nodded curtly, but it was plain that he wished to say nothing until they were alone, and after a long, thoughtful glance at him Darrell courteously bade him be seated and signed to the servants to give him food and wine. Then he dismissed them, and soon as they had gone Tom said quietly:

"They found him an hour ago. One of the farmhands saw his footprints in the mud by the stream, and on the path through the woods. Since that leads only here or to Conyngton, and it seemed unlikely that Shenfield would come to the Dower House, the fellow had the wit to seek him at the manor."

They were all silent for a space, thinking of the grim discovery which had awaited the unfortunate man. To Charity, remembering those moments of terror the previous night, it seemed that there was a strange justice in the fact that Jonas had died in the crashing ruins of the beautiful house he had coveted and wantonly destroyed. It was as though Conyngton, after waiting patiently through the lonely years, had finally taken its revenge.

"The news was brought to the Moat House," Tom

resumed after a little while, "and men have been sent to fetch Shenfield's body home." He paused for a moment, and then added deliberately, "Edward Taynton went with them."

Charity looked up sharply. "Mr. Taynton is here?"

"Does that surprise you?" Tom retorted with a touch of humour. "Yes, Miss Charity, he is here, and my father with him."

"Your father?" Linslade repeated in astonishment. "How the devil comes he into it?"

"It seems that Miss Catherine told Taynton I visited the house yesterday, and suggested that I must somehow be concerned in the disappearance of his wife and Miss Charity. Taynton, who has no kindness for me, thought this very likely, and sought news of me from my father, who, when all had been explained to him, resolved to come with Taynton to consult Jonas Shenfield. They had not long arrived when news came of Shenfield's death."

"What did you tell them, sir?" Charity asked with a frown.

"As little as possible," he replied frankly. "Merely that yesterday I escorted you, Miss Charity, from Plymouth to the Dower House, but that I know nothing of Mrs Taynton's present whereabouts. Fortunately, before they could question me more closely, word came that Shenfield had been found, and the whole household was thrown into confusion, but upon one point, at least, a decision was speedily reached. Both Taynton and your aunt demand your instant return to the Moat House."

Charity looked at Darrell. "What am I to do?"

He considered the question, frowning a little. "You

must go, I think," he said at length, "but I shall come with you, and be sure that I shall not let you remain there. Taynton's questions must be answered eventually, and the sooner 'tis done, the better." He glanced at Tom. "You will come with us, no doubt?"

"Aye!" Tom agreed with a laugh. "Some of those questions are bound to be directed at me, and I have no desire to be accused of playing a coward's part."

"I will come also!" Sir Richard said suddenly. "As Shenfield's brother-in-law I have as much right to be there as Taynton, and it may be that I can offer some practical aid. It would be wise, however, to agree before we leave this house upon what is supposed to have happened yesterday."

"It will indeed," Darrell agreed grimly. "Having so narrowly escaped one danger, we should be fools to blunder into another by way of heedlessness."

### III

At the Moat House, when they reached it, servants were hastily swathing the principal rooms and staircase in black cloth, and those who possessed it were already wearing mourning. The arrival of Charity and her companions at first went unnoticed in the general confusion, and when eventually a groom came to take charge of their horses, and a lackey to conduct them into the house, both stared in astonishment to see Sir Darrell Conyngton there at such a time. When they realised that the slender boy in grey who accompanied him was in fact Charity Shenfield, they passed beyond astonishment to complete stupefaction.

After a little delay the visitors were admitted to the

parlour, where Elizabeth Shenfield awaited them. Her eyes were red, but though her face was blotched and puffy from weeping, it was set in an expression of implacable hatred. Edward Taynton stood beside her chair, grim-faced and furious, while on the other side of the fireplace Ellen was seated, her eyes downcast, her fair hair already covered by the heavy black veil of widowhood. An elderly man, obviously her father, sat beside her; he looked troubled, as though he had been called upon to accept responsibilities far in excess of those which would normally have fallen upon him at the death of his daughter's husband.

Elizabeth's glance flicked indifferently past Tom and Sir Richard to fasten itself malevolently upon Darrell. She seemed about to address him, but then her attention was momentarily diverted by the sight of her niece. For a few seconds she stared, and then said in an outraged tone:

"Shameless wanton! Have you so little respect for your family that you come in that immodest guise to the house where your kinsman lies dead?"

"I had no choice, aunt, if I were to come at all," Charity replied quietly, "and Captain Pennan told me that you demanded my presence immediately." She went across to Ellen and laid a hand on her shoulder. "Child, what can I say?"

Slowly Ellen raised her face towards her. She was very pale, and still looked dazed with shock, but as her eyes met Charity's face the look in them silently acknowledged something which she could admit to no other living soul, not even her brother; the fact that to her, too, Jonas's death had come as a kind of release. For a long moment the dark eyes looked into the blue, and then Ellen bowed her head again.

"It is God's will," she said in a low voice.

Elizabeth uttered a harsh sound of anger and mockery. "The devil's work, more like!" she said bitterly, and turned an accusing gaze upon Darrell. "My son was murdered, wantonly cut down in the pride of his years, and I shall not rest until I have seen justice done! I know the enmity you bore towards him, Darrell Conyngton, and I marvel that you have the effrontery to enter this house of mourning as though no weight of guilt lay upon you!"

"Madam!" Darrell spoke quietly but very sternly. "You know well that the quarrel was not of my seeking. Your son chose to support a cause which I hate and despise with all my heart, but when the wars were over I would have lived in peace with him in spite of all which then lay between us. He would not have it so! I will not pretend to feel any sorrow at his passing, but I swear before God that I had no hand in his death."

"Lies!" she retorted implacably. "Blasphemous lies to cloak your own guilt and the guilt of that treacherous vixen beside you! I know not by what damnable trick you lured Jonas to his death, but that you did so lure him I am certain, as certain as I am of his salvation, and my own!"

"Mrs Shenfield!" Mr Pennan said protestingly, casting an anxious glance at Darrell. "Your natural grief provokes your tongue to a rashness which would be best forgotten. There is nothing to suggest that this tragedy was anything but a sad accident."

She looked at him with angry contempt. "Was it by accident that my son was at Conyngton?"

"As to that, madam, we shall never know," he replied soothingly, "but whatever took him there, it is not to be supposed that Sir Darrell had any hand in the disaster which caused his death. Even if he were there, which I think he was not . . ." He paused, and looked with apologetic inquiry at Darrell, who said curtly:

"No, sir, I was not! I was at the Dower House, as Sir Richard Linslade will tell you."

"That is so!" Linslade agreed promptly. "No doubt the servants will bear out what I say if it is considered necessary to question them, though, upon my life, *I* cannot see the need for it!"

"Enough of this!" Edward Taynton broke in angrily. "I saw how Jonas Shenfield died, and with respect, madam, no one save a bereaved and grieving mother would suggest that it was by aught but an act of God. No man could have caused his death, and no man, I think, could have saved him." He paused, and looked at Charity. "There are, however, other questions to be asked, and I think that you, mistress, are best fitted to answer them. Where is my wife?"

She faced him with an apparent composure, though in fact she felt less assured than she looked. She was prepared for the question but uncertain how far her reply would be believed.

"I do not know, sir," she said calmly. "We decided that it was better so, since what I do not know I cannot reveal."

"You decided!" he repeated. "By what right do *you* make any decision concerning my wife?"

"By the right of one who loves her," she replied boldly, "and who has witnessed the unkindness and indifference she suffered in your house."

He moved from his place beside Elizabeth's chair and came towards Charity until only a yard or so separated them. His plain, big-featured face was white with anger, the thin lips so tightly compressed that they were barely visible.

"Impertinent trollop!" he said deliberately. "You would be better advised not to remind me of your vile abuse of the manner in which I made you free of my house."

Darrell stepped forward and put Charity gently aside so that he confronted Taynton in her place. "You will ask Miss Shenfield's pardon for that insult," he said very quietly, "but first, tell us why you did make her free of your house."

Taynton scowled at him. Though by no means a small man, he was obliged to look up to meet the cold, hazel eyes, and this immediately put him at a disadvantage. He said rather warily: "To nurse my wife."

Darrell's brows lifted. "Are you sure the intention was not to remove Miss Shenfield from the protection of her friends in Conyngton St John so that her kinsman might more easily thrust her into marriage with his lackey Daniel Stotewood?" Taynton started, and flashed an angry, suspicious look at Elizabeth. Darrell shook his head. "Mrs Shenfield did not tell us that. Captain Pennan learned of it by chance, and made haste to warn Miss Shenfield of it."

Mr Pennan, who had listened to this exchange with astonished disapproval, said in a shocked tone: "Shenfield intended to marry his kinswoman to a servingman? You must be mistaken, Sir Darrell! It is unthinkable!"

"It is quite true, Father," Ellen said in a colourless voice. "Stotewood was to leave our service to become the landlord of an inn at a village near Kingsbridge. The inn was to be Charity's dowry. My husband boasted of it to me last night when I asked him how soon she would be coming home. Until then even *I* believed that Tom might be mistaken."

Taynton had quickly recovered his composure, and now attempted to justify both himself and the dead man. "It is a guardian's duty, Mr Pennan, to provide for the future of his ward. The young woman is penniless, and—"

"Do not discredit yourself even further, Taynton," Darrell broke in contemptuously. "You must know that Miss Shenfield has been betrothed to me for more than three years, and that only her kinsman's obstinate malice prevented our marriage. That you lent your aid to his vile schemes reflects no honour upon you!"

"So we are to speak of honour, are we?" Taynton said unpleasantly. "Then what of *my* honour, sir, which has been made a mockery of by this woman's meddling? I well know that my wife would have had neither the wit nor the spirit to plan unaided a flight with her lover, and were Charity Shenfield indeed the man whose dress she has chosen to assume, she would answer to me sword in hand!" A sudden thought seemed to strike him, and with a gleam of satisfaction in his eyes he turned to Tom. "As I live, there is no one other here who was closely concerned in the affair, and who *shall* answer to me. You, Captain Pennan!"

"I have never yet refused a challenge," Tom replied cheerfully, but Charity interrupted him without ceremony.

"Captain Pennan played no part in Sarah's flight, Mr Taynton, for our plans were already made when he came to me with his warning. Since I had already resolved to return to Conyngton St John after parting from Sarah, I was grateful to accept his company on the journey, but I met with him outside the town. You have no quarrel with him!"

For a few tense moments she wondered anxiously whether he would believe her. He looked suspiciously from Tom to her and back again, and perhaps upon consideration he was influenced a little by the fact that the Captain was nearly ten years younger than he and an even more experienced swordsman. Whatever the reason, he decided not to pursue the quarrel, but instead said savagely:

"My quarrel, mistress, is with the rogue who has seduced my wife, and though you cannot or will not tell me whither they have fled, be sure that I shall find them. And when I do, it will go hard with both of them!"

He bowed abruptly to Elizabeth and Ellen and then strode from the room, and they heard him shouting impatiently for his horse. Darrell looked at Mr Pennan.

"No purpose can be served by our remaining here," he said, "and it is plain that our presence is distressing to Mrs Shenfield. I say again that the quarrel between our families was not of my seeking, and I would be glad to see it at an end, the more so now that Miss Shenfield is about to become my wife." He turned to Elizabeth. "Madam, may we not bring this bitter enmity to an end?"

Slowly she turned her head to look up into his face. In her own, fury and grief and hatred were fused into an expression of the utmost malevolence. "Never, while my son's murder goes unpunished!" she said in a low, fierce voice. "His blood cries out to me for vengeance, and vengeance one day I will have. Now go, and take your paramour with you, and may you both be accursed in this world and damned beyond salvation in the next!"

For a moment he continued to regard her, and then with the smallest of shrugs he turned away. He took Charity by the arm and led her from the room, and Tom and Sir Richard followed them. Outside in the hall, Linslade said in a low voice:

"Conyngton, take Miss Charity to Dorringford. She may stay there with Beth until you can be wed. I had best remain here to lend what aid I can."

"I, also!" Tom agreed. "Ellen will be glad of my company, I think, and my father also may have need of me. There will be a deal of business to attend to, I do not doubt."

A servant was sent to fetch the horses, and Sir Richard bade Darrell and Charity farewell and returned to the parlour, but Tom went with them out on to the steps. As they waited there for the servant's return, Charity said softly:

"Is there any real danger of Mr Taynton finding Sarah and Mordisford before they can leave England?"

Tom shook his head, casting an experienced glance at the sky. "He would need to do so right speedily, for the wind has veered and is lessening, and if this weather holds it will not be many hours before they can put to sea. I think you need not fear for them, Miss Charity." He paused, regarding her with rueful humour. "I am not convinced, however, that you should have persuaded Taynton that he had no quarrel with me. I might have had the good fortune to set your cousin free."

"Or the misfortune, sir, to lose your own life," she retorted. "We value your friendship too greatly to let you risk that through any fault of ours, do we not, Darrell?"

"We do indeed," Darrell agreed seriously, "and we owe you a debt which we can never hope to repay, but of one thing, Captain Pennan, you may be sure. If ever there comes a time when you have need of friends, know that you will find them at Conyngton."

A groom came round the corner of the house leading the two horses, and Tom went to the head of Charity's mount as she swung into the saddle. Then, his hand still on the bridle, he looked up at her with a smile.

"Good fortune go with you, friend Charles," he said lightly. "You will have happiness now, I think, to make up for the slights and sorrows of the past."

She put out her hand to him. "I think so, too, friend Tom, but I shall never forget who made it possible."

He laughed and shook his head, grasping the proffered hand and then turning to take leave of Darrell. The horses moved off, and Tom stood for a few seconds looking after them, the laughter fading from his eyes. Then he sighed, and turned from the bright spring sunlight into the shadowed house again.

On the way along the track across the park, Charity drew rein and turned in the saddle to look back at the old house, half hidden now by trees and by the ruined wall beside the moat; at the moat itself, which still had power to evoke a bitter memory. She might see them again, might even, in years to come, enter the house once more, but now she had a sense of leaving it for ever. She went without regret, for she had never known real happiness there.

Darrell had halted and was watching her, studying the dark, dauntless face which was so dear to him, and because their spirits were so closely attuned he knew without the need for question what she was feeling then. His own heart was filled with deep thankfulness and joy, for the two things most precious to him on earth, Charity and Conyngton, were safe in his possession at last.

At length Charity's gaze left the distant house and returned to him. Her thoughts were echoing his, for she, too, had realised that with Jonas dead there need be no flight into exile, no roaming through foreign lands. The time of waiting was over, and though many hardships might lie ahead, and many years pass before the King came into his own again, these things would be easier to bear because they would face them together. She smiled, and put out her hand to him as the horses moved slowly on, and side by side they rode to meet the challenge of the future.

# Sylvia Thorpe

*Sparkling novels of love and conquest set against the colorful background of historic England. Here are stories you will savor word by word, page by spell-binding page into the wee hours of the night.*

| | | |
|---|---|---|
| ☐ BEGGAR ON HORSEBACK | 23091-0 | 1.50 |
| ☐ CAPTAIN GALLANT | Q2709 | 1.50 |
| ☐ FAIR SHINE THE DAY | 23229-8 | 1.75 |
| ☐ THE GOLDEN PANTHER | 23006-6 | 1.50 |
| ☐ THE RELUCTANT ADVENTURESS | P2578 | 1.25 |
| ☐ ROGUE'S COVENANT | 23041-4 | 1.50 |
| ☐ ROMANTIC LADY | Q2910 | 1.50 |
| ☐ THE SCANDALOUS LADY ROBIN | Q2934 | 1.50 |
| ☐ THE SCAPEGRACE | P2663 | 1.25 |
| ☐ THE SCARLET DOMINO | 23220-4 | 1.50 |
| ☐ THE SILVER NIGHTINGALE | P2626 | 1.25 |
| ☐ THE SWORD AND THE SHADOW | 22945-9 | 1.50 |
| ☐ SWORD OF VENGEANCE | 23136-4 | 1.50 |
| ☐ TARRINGTON CHASE | Q2843 | 1.50 |